C000161831

The Smile of the Unknown Mariner

VINCENZO CONSOLO

The Smile of the Unknown Mariner

Translated with an afterword by
Joseph Farrell

CARCANET

First published in Great Britain in 1994
by Carcanet Press Limited
208-12 Corn Exchange, Manchester M4 3BQ

Translation copyright © 1994 Joseph Farrell

Translated from the Italian
Il sorriso dell'ignoto marinaio
© 1976 Guilio Einaudi editore s.p.a., Turin

The right of Joseph Farrell to be identified
as the translator of this work
has been asserted by him
in accordance with the
Copyright, Designs and Patents Acts of 1988
All rights reserved

A CIP catalogue record for this book
is available from the British Library

ISBN 1 85754 051 4

The publisher acknowledges financial assistance
from the Arts Council of England

Set in 10pt Bembo by Bryan Williamson, Frome
Printed and bound in Great Britain
by Short Run Press, Exeter

Funded by
THE
ARTS
COUNCIL
OF ENGLAND

For Caterina

Contents

Antonel of Sicily, a man of such light...
Gismondo Santi, *Cronica rimata*

The play on resemblances is in Sicily a
delicate and sensitive test, an
instrument of knowledge (...) The
portraits of Antonello 'resemble.' They
constitute the very idea, the alpha of
resemblance (...) Whom does the Unknown
Man of the Mandralisca Museum resemble?
Leonardo Sciascia, *L'Ordine delle somiglianze*

ONE

The Smile of the Unknown Mariner

PREAMBLE

The sea voyage of Enrico Pirajno, Baron of Mandralisca, from Lipari to Cefalu, bearing the canvas with the portrait of an unknown man by Antonella da Messina. The painting, recovered from an inset panel in a cabinet on the premises of the apothecary, Carnevale, is slightly disfigured by two crossed scratches on the forward part of the sitter's smiling lips. According to the people of Lipari, the apothecary's daughter, Catena, still unmarried at the ripe age of twenty-five, enraged (there was, they report, a particularly oppressive scirocco blowing that day) by the man's intolerable smile, inflicted on him two blows with the agave spine she used for punching holes in the linen pulled taut over her embroidery frame. This was believed to be why the apothecary Carnevale sold the work to Baron Mandralisca; he had the good of his daughter at heart, and wished to see her back behind the counter serenely engaged on her embroidery, picking out the patterns for which she had such a knack (in a trice she could do you a set of initials, produce the most elaborate flourishes, arabesques, frills, run up lines or strings of dots and stops...). In a shaft of light falling from the lunette in the side wall, between the counter and the shelves loaded with flasks, jars, ointment pots, cruets, boxes, crucibles, she herself remained barely visible to the darting glances of the young men passing backwards and forwards on the Strada San Bartolomeo (the beautiful, unattainable Catena remained a mystery; was she concealing some unconfessable love of her own or merely taking delight in playing havoc with the suppressed passions of others?).

*   *   *

And now the great island came into view. The lamps on the towers along the coast were red and green, they swayed and fell from view to reappear as bright as before. Once it entered the waters of the gulf, the vessel ceased rolling. In the channel between Tindari and Vulcano, the waves whipped up by the scirocco had battered it from every side. Throughout the night Mandralisca, standing near the forward railing, had heard nothing but the roar of the waters, the creak and snap of the sails, and a rattling sound that approached and receded with the wind. And now that the vessel advanced, silent and stately, within the bay, on a calmer, more slow-running sea, he clearly heard behind him the same rattle, drawn out and unchanging. The sound of breathing which, with choking noises and rasping coughs, came painfully from rigid, contracted lungs, forcing its way along the windpipe and issuing, with a low groan, from a mouth that he imagined open as wide as possible. In the lantern's faint light, Mandralisca made out a brightness which might have been the gleam of eyes in the darkness.

He turned his gaze back to the skies and the stars, to the great island ahead, to the lamps on the towers. Keeps built of sandstone and mortar displayed their high, crenellated finery on the sheer rock that takes the force of the sea winds and waves – the towers of Calava and Calanovella, of Lauro and Gioisa, of Brolo...

Out on the balcony of the castle of Lancia stands Lady Bianca, feeling sick. She sighs and vomits, peering at the distant horizon. The wind of Swabia tears her apart. The Emperor Frederick of Swabia confides to his falcon:

> O God, what madness was in me
> When you made me depart
> From where I had great dignity;
> I pay a bitter price,
> Like snow I melt away...

Behind the lamps, in the centre of the bay stood cities once, under the olive groves: Abacena and Agatirno, Alunzio and Calacte, Alesa... cities in which Mandralisca would have knelt down to claw at the soil with his bare hands, had he been sure of finding a vase, a lantern or even just a coin. Now those cities are no more

than names, sounds, dreams full of yearning. And he clasped to
his chest the painting wrapped in waxed canvas he'd brought
from Lipari; he tested with his fingers its solidity and hardness,
relished the subtle aromas of camphor and mustard with which it
was impregnated after so many years in the apothecary's shop.

But these scents were suddenly overwhelmed by others, waft-
ing from the land, stronger than the scirocco, heavy and powerful
with garlic, fennel, oregano, bay leaf and calamint. With them
came the cries and beating wings of the seagulls. A great fan-like
brightness rose up from the depths of the sea; the stars disap-
peared, the lights from the towers grew faint.

The rattling sound had changed into a dry, stubborn cough.
Then Mandralisca saw, in the dawn's sharp light, a naked man
bent over backwards, dark and desiccated as an olive tree, his outstretched arms clinging to the foreyard, his head thrown back as
he struggled to open his throat and release some clot gnawing at
his chest. A woman was drying his forehead and neck. She
became aware of the gentleman, removed her shawl and wrapped
it round the sick man's thighs. He was racked by a last, terrible fit
of coughing and immediately ran to the rail. He turned pale, his
eyes dilated and staring, and he pressed a cloth over his mouth.
His wife helped him lie down on the deck, among the ship's
tackle.

'Stone disease,' said a voice which seemed to come from inside
the Baron's ear. Mandralisca found himself face to face with a
man, who smiled strangely – the ironic, caustic, bitter smile of
one who has seen much and knows much, who is aware of the
present and senses the future, who strives to defend himself from
the pain of knowledge and the continual temptation of compassion.
His eyes were small and sharp under arched eyebrows. Two deep
wrinkles scored his hard face at the mouth's corners, as though to
mark and emphasise that smile. The man was dressed as a sailor,
with cloth bonnet, jacket and flared trousers. On closer examina-
tion, however, he turned out to be an unusual mariner: he lacked
the somnolent detachment and dull alienation characteristic of
someone who had spent his life at sea, but had the alertness of a
landsman who has lived in the midst of men and their affairs. An
observer might have noted in him an aristocratic bearing.

'Stone disease,' continued the mariner. 'He's a pumice quarry-man from Lipari. There are hundreds like him on this island. They're lucky if they reach forty. The doctors have no idea what to do with them, so they come here to implore the Black Madonna of Tindari for a miracle. Apothecaries and herbalists treat them with poultices and infusions and make a fat profit. These same doctors slice them open once they're dead, to study those whitened lungs which have turned as hard as the stone they sharpen their little knives on. What is there to look for? It's the stone, the pumice dust. They'll never understand that everything depends on not swallowing the stuff.'

And here, noting a mixture of pain and surprise in the Baron's expression, he smiled his bitter, ironic smile. The Baron, still intent on the mariner's speech, had been trying to remember where and when he'd seen him before. He was so certain of this that he would willingly have wagered his estate at Colombo or the *Tuna Vendor* vase from his collection. But *where* had he seen him?

Under the man's piercing glance, however, his thoughts returned to the quarryman. Beyond Canneto, towards the west, a dazzling white mountain called Pelato rises from the sea. There a vast army of men, a black swarm of tarantulas and beetles, labours under a sun as fierce as that of Morocco, cutting into the porous rock with their pickaxes. Bent double under their baskets, they emerge from holes, caves, galleries in the rock; they slither and slide along narrow planks, bridges stretching into the sea, towards the boats. As these images arose, Mandralisca strove to repress others which were just then, by some unexplained associ-ation or counterpoint, forcing their way to the surface (flocks of birds migrating towards Africa under a stormy sky; green snails leaving silvery trails on the rock; high swaying palm trees offer-ing a fleeting glimpse of the vulva of the spathes with their Easter-white inflorescences . . .). And then, to the Baron's acute dismay, before this man, who was both investigator and judge, his own various studies presented themselves. Arranged volume by volume, each with its title, publisher and year of publication; these were the monographs which – in ordinary circumstances – gave the Baron quiet delight, pride and a certain satisfaction: his *Catalogue of the Birds Native to or in Passage in the Aeolian Islands, Catalogue of the Terrestrial and Fluvial Molluscs of the Madonie Mountains and Parts Adjacent Thereto, Catalogue and Fecundation of Palm Trees.*

The mariner read, and smiled, with ironical commiseration.

From the stern came the noise of shouting and of the anchor chains being unwound and lowered into the water. The ship had arrived at Oliveri, under the rock of Tindari. The mariner left the Baron and walked off, with a sprightly step, towards the fore-mast.

The sun's rays above the horizon lit up the massive rock with its ancient theatre, gymnasium and sanctuary perched on top, the whole form rising sheer out of the great wastes of land and water. The beach was an embroidered pattern of golds and enamels. In sinuous tongues, circles, zigzags, the yellow sand formed basins, canals, lakes, inlets. The waters contained every shade of blue and green. Reeds, rushes, mosses, slimy filaments grew all around; fat fish swam and slow seagulls and lazy herons waded in those waters. The mother-of-pearl of mussels and shellfish, and the white of limed starfish glistened on the sand. Small boats with sails still furled on the mast floated motionless on the still waters among the dunes, like the flotsam and jetsam of tides. A heavy, humid air hung over the beach, with a dormant scirocco visible in some low, frayed twists of cloud. What cosmic event, what earthquake had cast into the sea the highest peaks of the rock together with the ancient city that once nestled there? What lost treasures lay under those green waters, those sands! Wholly unknown herbs, unimagined vegetation, encrustations covering the shoulders, arms, thighs of Venuses and Dioscuri!

So Adelasia, carved alabaster queen, the lace frills rigid over her sleeves, waited impassively for the convent to disintegrate. 'Who is there, in the name of God?' – the centuries-old, solitary Abbess's question echoed round the cloister, until it lost itself in the cells, the huge chambers, the deserted passageways. 'Did His Grace the Archbishop send you?' And outside all was emptiness, a whirlwind of days and suns and waters, gusts of spiralling winds, crumbling sandstone walls, tumbling dunes, hills, falls of stone, waste. The thistle emerges, wrenches round, offers at last its trembling, diaphanous flower to the white donkey's hollow eye. A light that burns, bites, smoothes sides, angles, points, lightens shades and stains, abolishes colour – it welds together wisps of grass, whitens stray branches and, beyond the moving plain of fish-scales and horizons, dissolves and reshapes the massive forms.

Now, above the rock, on the cliff's edge, the little sanctuary sheltered the *nigra Bizantina*, the Virgin Most Gracious, encased in the veil's perfect triangle, resplendent with garnets, pearls and aquamarines, unsuffering Queen, silent Sibyl, Libyan ebony, with the unchanging gesture of the hand clasping the stem of the three-lilied silver sceptre.

'Mind your own damn business,' Mandralisca ordered Rosario.

The servant had only just appeared, his head still enveloped in veils of sleep, to beg his master to go and rest.

'Your Excellency, is this how Christian folk behave – you stay outside all night long, on your feet, with that bit of wood stuck to your breast as though you were giving suck?'

'Rosario, I known what I've got here. If you want to carry on snoring, snore away! Like the beast you are.'

'Sleep, Excellency! I haven't so much as closed an eye, God strike me dead if I tell a lie. Every last one of those lobster claws I was sucking away at yesterday evening ended up in the sea.'

'Yes, together with every last piece of flesh inside the shell those four claws once carried along the sea-floor, Rosario, not to mention the caper sauce they were so nicely soused in.'

'Yes, Excellency. Exquisite. What a shame!'

'To say nothing of what washed it all down.'

'Yes, Excellency. Julep wine. But I was saying...'

'Rosario, I understand. Go back to sleep.'

'Yes, Your Excellency.'

The unknown mariner, standing upright in the crow's nest, blew the triton shell three times, and the sound, echoing from the rocks, returned three times to the sailing ship. A flock of coots and seagulls rose up from the beach, while crows and ravens swooped down from the cliffs. A four-oared boat set out from the Oliveri shoreline. From every corner of the decks and up from the holds, groups of pilgrims appeared. There were dishevelled women travelling barefoot in fulfilment of a vow, old women with baskets and bags as well as children in their arms, men laden with sacks, barrels and demi-johns. They were bringing wine from Pianoconte, malvasia from Canneto, ricotta cheeses from Vulcano, wheat from Salina, capers from Acquacalda and Quattropani. And each one carried, high aloft, pink or flesh-coloured limbs made of wax – heads, legs, breasts or secret organs – painted blue or black in various spots to mark the disfiguring growths, swellings, scars and other ills. The pumice-stone quarryman now wore a hooded goatswool cloak and carried a candle as tall as himself. Two complete, pear-shaped *caciocavallo* cheeses, shining with the oil smeared over their surface, hung over his wife's breast, attached to a cord that cut into her neck. The rowing-boat touched the wooden side of the sailing ship, and the pilgrims, calling to each other and shouting, crowded on the gangway to disembark.

A long boat with a cargo of clay pots, vases, amphoras, jugs, plates and pitchers, all from the factories of Marina di Patti, put out from the shore. It was carrying, lined up on deck at the prow, four white marble statues of toga-clad consuls, leaning forward like captains, one with a head and three without, each reflected upside down in the water. Behind these, other dismembered marbles, and, still further behind, miniature trees from the nurseries of Mazzara – orange, lemon, bergamot, mandarin, cedar and lime – were lined up in their plant pots. These bushes, which adorned the stairwells, winter gardens, galleries and pavilions of palaces and courts in Palermo, Naples and Caserta, Versailles and Venice, grew luxuriantly in Mazzara on account of the heat and humours of this land which resembled a quarry, hollow, ditch, groin, female organ (Baron?!). The long boat glided slowly, silently below the sailing ship where Mandralisca stood, giving him the opportunity to observe at leisure.

The marbles behind the statues represented *the most elegant Greek workmanship, depicting two feet with legs up to the thighs of a youthful male nude, with a skilfully decorated altar in white alabaster marble, to the left. A further two large items of marble statuary together form the colossal torso of a man: in one of these items the decorated, bas-relief armour is clearly visible, and among the features one can observe the breast-plate with crest of matted hair, such as can be found on many medallions. A highly worked strap hangs from the right shoulder over the chest. On the left shoulder the pallium intended as cover for both shoulders is elegantly picked out. Over the belly, two hippogryphs appear. The other piece of marble was the remainder of the armour, i.e. the fibulae and the breast plate, reaching down to the loin-cloth over the thighs, which themselves present divers incisions. The breast plates depicted small heads of various animals and some humans. The existence of these fragments in the Tindari area has caused some to conjecture that they formed part of a statue of the Dioscuri, described by the poets in military attire.* Ah God! what beauty! But where was that thieving long boat bound for? For white, thalassic, rocky Syracuse, or for red, sultanic, palmy Palermo? A pirate; the Baron would have loved to play the pirate and attack that boat at the head of some rascally band. He'd haul it off to his own beloved port of the Vascio at Cefalu, nestling beneath the rocks, teeming with shoals of mullet, on salt waters made fresh by currents from the springs and founts of Arethusa. And then he'd have shown Biscari, Asmundo Zappala, Canon Alessi, perhaps even the Cardinal, as well as Pepoli, Bellomo and even Landolina!

The procession of the other pilgrims, who had come from the countryside and towns of Val Demone to Tindari for the September feast, snaked along high up in the rocks, following the winding road that led from Oliveri to the shrine. As they climbed they chanted incomprehensible songs, which ricocheted from the front to the rear of the group, criss-crossing in the middle to create a tangle of sound, but then, after countless endeavours and detours, seeming to fuse, to become one strong, clear chant which grew under its own force and swelled as the procession proceeded towards the shrine.

A beautiful girl with raven-black hair and green, flashing eyes, seated in the long boat with the others, rose to her feet when the song's echo reached her and, swaying softly, struck up a chant of her own: a vile, obscene chant which the prisoners over there in Lipari, clinging to the iron bars of the castle, intoned in the evening. Her mother, in the attempt to prevent her and stop her mouth with her hand, dropped a votive wax head into the water, where it floated a moment, its pure, white forehead still visible, before sinking from sight.

THE BARON ENRICO PIRAJNO DI MANDRALISCA
AND THE BARONESS HIS WIFE
REQUEST THE PLEASURE OF YOUR COMPANY
THE EVENING OF 27 OCTOBER 1852
IN THEIR TOWN HOUSE
TO ENJOY WITH THEM THE UNVEILING
OF A NEW ADDITION TO THEIR COLLECTION
AND TO GIVE THEM THE HONOUR OF WAITING ON YOU

After making the rounds of the town, devoting the entire morning to climbing up and down external and internal staircases with this piece of paper in his white gloved hand, Rosario had orders to proceed to Castelluccio: across the Santa Barbara hill, down the Sant'Oliva valley, clambering back up, making little detours and occasionally breaking into a run to avoid the dogs that barked menacingly as he passed, picking up the path again in the middle of wild gorse and bramble patches, calling down the most wicked of curses on the head and heart of Count Baucina who – at this time of the year, long after the grapes were harvested and everyone else had moved back to town – had remained where he was, roosted among the rocks of Castelluccio.

On the way back, he called in at Quattroventi. The mills groaned as they ground the wheat transported that morning by a line of mules linked by iron rings. Hens scratched, and clouds of brightly coloured flies swarmed on the piles of dung, among the fetlocks. Wasps and mosquitoes buzzed drunkenly above the trickles of water clogged by must from the millstones. The peasants came out from the warehouse to stare open-mouthed at Rosario, resplendent in his footman's livery. At the Terra gate, in front of the smithy, the blacksmith burned the hoof of a mule, and the stench of scalded flesh hung in the air. Discomfitted, Rosario set off down the Strada Regale. In this narrow alley he found himself set upon by fishmongers. Standing with back and one foot against the wall, baskets at their side, they deafened him with cries, with jeers, with blandishments. One ran after him to thrust under his nose a rotting grey mullet, packed in a dripping handful of seaweed.

'I've made all my purchases, I've made all my purchases, thank you,' said Rosario, pushing the man's arm away with a fastidious white index finger.

Rosario was weary, slightly sick but principally irritated at the Baron's bizarre whimsy.

'Lucky man, you're a lucky man, Rosario. Your ship's come in!' said a deep, cavernous voice which appeared to come from beneath his feet, just when those flat feet in little shoes and fleshy calves clothed in white moved past the small, barred and grated windows at street level, under the Grand Hostelry.

'It's your boat that's come in, isn't it? Down there with no worries, no problems,' snarled Rosario in reply. A loud salvo of oaths like artillery fire was aimed at his back as he retreated.

Near the apothecary's shop, a notorious den of idlers and gossips, so as not to advertise his rage and humiliation for their entertainment, he drew in his stomach and tucked it in under his tightened belt, clamped his upper lip firmly on to the still trembling lower lip, reined in his wandering glance and fixed it unwaveringly on the street ahead. Emerging on to the square in front of the Cathedral, he sighed with relief at the sight of that open space and light, and could not resist stopping at the kiosk to ask Pasquale for a glass of water with a drop of aniseed.

He dropped on to the seat, letting his arms rest on the cabinet and emitting a long 'Aaahhhhh.'

'Tired, Rosario?' came Pasquale's question.

With his friend he gave free rein to his ill humour.

'You'd think it was a christening, or a wedding, or something. Imagine throwing a party for a section of the side of a medicine cabinet, bought from some herbalist in Lipari. Painted, so he says, by someone by the name of 'Ntonello, from Messina.'

'From Messina! And when did anything worthwhile ever come from Messina? Bunch of drivellers, that's all they are. What's the Baron up to? If you want art, you've got it right here,' he said, waving grandly in the direction of the Cathedral. 'Our Almighty Patron over the high altar, the Most Holy Saviour, inlaid with gold and precious stones, and all done by us, the people of Cefalu.'

The shadows of the palm tree foliage fell sheer on to the roadway, making a crown around the base of the trunks. The blind organist passed through the Gate of the Kings, reached out beyond

the portico, descended the steep stairway away from the limestone bishops at the top, and beat with his cane the scowling face
of the stone lion perched above the basin of the dried up fountain.
From behind the church's twin towers, the bells could be seen
flickering: the midday chime, shimmering in the still air like the
zigzagging arches that wove in and out along the façade, rang out
through Giudecca Gate as far as Presidiana, up the Saraceni slope
to the first outcrop of the Rock, through Piscaria Gate to the boats
floating motionless within the harbour and as far as Santa Lucia.

Baron Mandralisca's drawing-room had taken on the appearance of a museum. The ebony and ivory miniatures, the Louis
XVI sofas, the crushed velvet canapés and armchairs, the inlaid
tondi, the Malvica medallions had all been removed and piled up
in the entrance hall or in the study, leaving the marks of their
lengthy stay in that room clearly visible on the silk-covered walls.
All that remained were the consoles with *peluche* surfaces, on
which rested China blue and gold vases, as well as green and
white, turquoise and pink *potiches* from Cochin-China. And
Saxony and Meissen porcelain, alabaster fruits, Jacob-Petit
pheasants, hens and cockerels, gilded bronze clocks and wax
flowers in glass cases.

The guests remained standing, with the exception of the
elderly ladies who occupied, with the expanse of their crinolines,
the few chairs and the one pouffe placed in the centre of the room.
The young ladies and gentlemen were grouped around the piano,
where Baronessa Maria Francesca accompanied the uncertain
warblings of her niece, Annetta.

Carmine Papa, the ploughman poet, who was taken along to
all the festivities in the houses of the nobility by his supporters
and patrons, Baron Maria and Cavaliere Culotta, kept himself
apart from the others but was always as ready to perform as a
Barberia piano-organ. He had all his poems by heart, so they had
only to throw a title at him and off he went, never faltering, never
missing a beat. The favourite was always the romance of Ruggero,
the Norman king who set sail from Naples with his fleet but was
overtaken at sea off Salerno by a tempest and made a vow to
Christ the Saviour to raise a temple in His honour if he reached
land safe and sound. Having landed safely at Cefalu, he had the

Cathedral constructed there, the object of esteem and admiration to this day in every part of the globe. Carmine would start off quietly and gently, but when he got to the miracle, he rose to a fine crescendo, turned red in the face and ended up declaiming at the top of his voice:

> After the tempest and the terror,
> The miracle was worked indeed.
> At Cefalu the king was landed
> And there his beating heart fell still.
> At once he spoke with fire and fervour:
> I'll make a vow, my Saviour Christ,
> To build a temple on this spot
> In gratitude for God's good favour.

'What utter nonsense, nonsense!' muttered Mandralisca under his breath. He could never digest that legend of King Ruggero, artfully inflated by the bishop and the clergy. The fact was that, on the basis of that vow and of the subsequent Deed of 1145, by which the founder of the Sicilian monarchy generously endowed the Cathedral to ensure the repose of the souls of his father Count Ruggero and of his mother Adelasia, the bishop had wielded power for centuries, even after the suppression of the feudal system, imposing on the people of Cefalu levies, dues, abuses, injustices and every manner of vexation... (capitation on every beast of burden delivering cereals to Cefalu; the right of slaughter, that is, a tax on every cow, pig or other animal slaughtered; a tithe on limestone; tithe on all earthenware goods; tithe on all orchard produce and on every clove of garlic; a levy of one twelfth of total value on all must wines; custom duties by land and sea, that is, on anchorage, berthing and stallage; a tithe on fish, that is, on all sardines, anchovies and scaly fish; land tax; veto on the sale of snow, this latter being the exclusive preserve of the episcopal palace...). It was clear that those two fools, Maria and Culotta, who protected the ploughman poet Papa (could it have been on account of the name?) were hand-in-glove with the bishop, previously Proto and now this new man, Ruggero the Blond. Ignoramuses! Had they never taken the trouble to read his monograph (*On the Pretensions of the Bishopric of Cefalu – Brief Considerations*, by

Enrico Pirajno, Baron of Mandralisca. Palermo; publisher M.A. Console, Via S Giuseppe di Arimathea. 1844), wherein it was demonstrated beyond all question that the bishop was not invested with a barony but merely with a seigniory of the first rank?

Salvatore Spinuzza, still carrying on his forehead and wrists the marks of the tortures – the angelic torture, the headscrew, the thumbscrew – inflicted on him by King Ferdinand's police, stood apart from the company, haughty and taciturn, his arms folded, his blue eyes and blond goatee beard pointing upwards, flanked on either side, as by Saints Cosmas and Damian, by the two Botta brothers, Nicola and Carlo. And behind, as though to guard their backs, the other two companions, Guarnera and Maggio. Everyone ignored Spinuzza, everyone studiously avoided him, except for the master of the house and his relatives Agnello and Baron Bordonaro. And except for Giovanna Oddo.

The Duke of Alberi, with his deep resonant voice, held court among the noblest ladies and gentlemen of Cefalu society. He talked of the hydra of anarchy, of the disturbers of the peace, of young men whose heads were filled with all manner of nonsense and tomfoolery, dangerous enemies of His Majesty the King (Whom God Protect) and of Holy Mother Church. The Lord Lieutenant, the good Prince of Satriano, was too kind-hearted, too full of the milk of human kindness, wasting all that time and money with trials and imprisonment (Dear God, had he not learned anything from the riots of '48?): the gallows, immediately, no second chances, that was the only remedy!

Giovanna Oddo turned to Spinuzza with a pleading, painful look. Salvatore lost his composure, tossed his head to restore to its place the one blond curl that had fallen over his forehead, and returned Giovanna's glance. The merest trace of a smile played on his lips.

Giovanna was already in tears as if she were already standing – Mother of God – before that beloved body, dangling from a rope like a bundle of rags.

'Idiot!' whispered her mother, digging her elbow into her with all her strength. 'Have you no shame? Go out on to the balcony, dry your eyes. We'll sort this out when we get home.'

Elisabetta and Giuseppina, sisters of the Botta brothers, detached themselves from the wall in unison. They crossed the drawing room as though floating above the floor and linked hands in front of Giovanna Oddo. Held at the waist by the two graceful arms of the two angels, Giovanna allowed herself to be led to the balcony.

'Ah, what poor bargains these young girls strike nowadays,' pontificated the Duke of Alberi, as though continuing his speech.

Donna Salvina Oddo threw a deep sigh. 'May I compliment you, Duke, on your monument?' she said quickly, to change the subject.

The Duke, flattered, launched into a detailed description of the magnificent tomb he had had constructed in the cemetery and unveiled and blessed the previous Friday.

'I wouldn't dare tell you how much it cost me! All in polychrome marbles, with ribs and arabesques intertwined, following the style of Pampillonia at Gibilmanna, with half bust, coat of arms, and the inscription... ANTE DECESSUM TUMULUM POSUI etcetera, etcetera.

'I planted seven acres of manna,' said Count Baucina loudly to the now ageing and slightly deaf Cavaliere Invidiato. 'And I dug up ten acres for a new vineyard.'

'Be grateful it was not your grave you were digging,' the Duke of Alberi said to him, before turning back to Signora Oddo.

'A beautiful ceremony indeed. An intimate, religious occasion. Only close family, the Confraternity for a Holy Death, with Father Mitrato there to administer the blessing and deliver the sermon.'

The time had come for the visit to the museum. With Baron Mandralisca as guide, they made a tour of the paintings which had been arranged in twin rows along the walls. They listened distractedly to warm words on Bevelacqua's *Dawn over Cefalu*, on the intensity of expression in Novelli's *Saint Anne*, on the subtle perspective in the *Last Supper* by the school of Ruzzolone, where the figures were so rotund and chubby, so evidently replete as to make it seem indeed a last supper, but one whose beginning was unknown and which had proceeded with an unending stream of plates of macaroni with bolognese sauce. And so on, past the Byzantine panels, the unknown Sicilians, the Neapolitans and Spaniards, until they reached the painting of the beguiling young woman offering to the lips of a wizened old man the pink nipple of a milk-white breast which peeped shyly into the light from a dark background.

'I'm coming, mother,' said Signorina Micciche, as though she had suddenly understood that some piece of business urgently required her attention. And she split off from the group, together with the Misses Barranco and Pernice, and that pert little coquette, Signorina Coco.

'Madonna! This heat! Let's go onto the balcony,' and 'Goodness, what have I done with my glove,' said other voices, as they were escorted to the case with the Greek vases.

In addition to the *Tuna Vendor* or pictures of languid matrons reclining while flustered chambermaids assisted them in their *toilette*, there were red-and-black vases depicting shameless and lubricious fauns displaying all the erect evidence of recent ruttings, their arms round the waist or at the back of certain prancing nymphs, whom they were striving to lead off, poor things, to some unseen spot, and other scenes of flight and capture, of ecstatic maidens facing garlanded youths, staff in hand, whose intentions were unclear.

The men indulged in nudges, winks, *risqué* interpretations delivered *sotto voce*, while the Baron droned on about the age and provenance of these relics of antiquity.

At the stands and cases devoted to lamps and coins, where the Baron let himself go with an unending series of dates, of place-names, of symbols and values, those four or five who, out of esteem for the man or out of courtesy remained close to him, heard a string of such words as Motya, Panormus, Lipara, Litra, Nummary, Decadrachma.

The servants entered carrying trays weighed down with croissants with butter and tuna paste, sesame seed biscuits, Santa Caterina cakes, pralines, fritters, *petits fours*, sweetmeats with cloves, *choux*. Rosario, with a captain's skill, led the assault on the various groups of guests, giving instructions with his eyes and with one hand, leaving the other free to scratch under the wig which was making his head itch. But his real enemy, the portrait under the wrap, was there in the middle of the room, placed on a high pedestal, flanked by two squat, candle-bearing Moors on curlicue columns. Passing in front of it, Rosario threw it a surly look.

The voices of other enemies, more alive and more starved, came in from the balconies which opened onto Strada Badia. Like dogs which had followed the scent of the sweets drifting through the air, the boys of the town emerged from the Gonzaga court- yard, from the Ferraresi, Siracusani and Monte di Pieta alley- ways, congregated under the balcony and began to yell:

'Rosario, Rosario, come out here, Rosario!'

They took up the chant:

> Drunken Martina, jolly Lucia
> Every dog will have its bitch
> So hey ho! which bitch is mine tonight?

'These scum,' murmured Rosario as he moved swiftly to close the windows.

> Pierce the pumpkin with the rod,
> My lovely's here, a roll of drums
> In! out! and watch her come.

The chants in the street grew louder and more excited as the singers danced, clapped their hands and threw stones at the windows.

'Rosario,' ordered the Baroness Maria Francesca, 'send Rosalia down with a tray.'

While the guests went on sipping their malvasia and Salaparuta sherry, the Baron made a sign to Rosario to light the twelve can- dles in the hands of the Moors. He moved over to the stand and in the sudden silence, removed the cloth covering the painting.

There appeared the image of the head and shoulders of a man. From the gloomy green, nocturnal background, redolent of long nights of fear and incomprehension, the radiant face thrust itself forward. A dark garment separated the light tone of the strong neck from the chest, while the close-fitting headgear, of the same colour as the rest of the outfit, divided the forehead in two. The man was of exactly that age at which reason, having reached shore safely after the shipwreck of youth, has forged itself into a steel blade that will become, with continual use, ever more lucid and sharp. The shadow of a two days' beard on the face gave greater prominence to the wide cheek bones, to the clean, perfect line of the pointed nose, to the lips, to the expression. The tiny, pitch black pupils peeped out sternly from the corners of the eyes and the lips themselves barely puckered into a smile. The whole expression was fixed forever in a mark of irony, that subtle, changing, fleeting, sublime veil of acrid reserve with which gifted beings cover compassion. Were it not for that half smile, the face would have fallen into the laboured repose of seriousness and gloom, would have settled for the mere absence of pain; without the smile, it would have lost all composure, would have been contorted into open, sarcastic, heartless laughter or into the mechanically liberating laughter common to all mankind.

The subject, with his small, intense eyes fixed each of the company squarely in the eye, wherever they moved, smiled at each of them, ironically, leaving each with a feeling of unease.

From the Ossuna Gate at that moment came the sound of guns firing and dogs barking. It was the patrol, which, in these unsettled times, shot at every imagined shadow they detected outside the city gates. Spinuzza became restless and felt a tremor run up his spine.

In the silence which followed those shots, the smile on the face of the man on the pedestal seemed to grow stronger. Mandralisca stared repeatedly at him, adjusting his pince-nez and stroking his beard with his hand, as though he too were viewing him for the first time. He turned to the company and, eyes fixed on the majolica flooring, began in a thoughtful monotone:

'It makes my heart glad to express the hope... I am convinced ... I am indeed strongly of the opinion that we have here a work by the hand of Antonella da Messina...'

He suddenly raised his eyes, struck his forehead with his hand and exclaimed: 'Rosario, the unknown mariner!'

Rosario threw out his arms, and his expression altered as though he had before him a person speaking Turkish. There was a burst of loud laughter in the chamber. The Duke of Alberi, as straight as a rod from behind, but with a few buttons undone on his evening jacket to accommodate the bulge he triumphantly carried in front, addressed Mandralisca loudly in his fluting voice. 'Baron, who is that fellow smiling at?' pointing at the portrait.

'At crazy fools like you and me, at imbeciles everywhere,' replied the Baron.

APPENDIX ONE

Letter from Enrico Pirajno, Baron of Mandralisca, to Baron Andrea Bivona to serve as preface to the Catalogue of Terrestrial and Fluvial Molluscs of the Madonie Mountains and Parts Adjacent Thereto *(Palermo, Oretea publishers, 204 Via dell'Albergaria, 1840).*

My illustrious friend,

Since the exercise of your professional duties did not permit you to accompany me on my visit to the Nebrodi Mountains, I hasten to satisfy your curiosity by forwarding this catalogue wherein you will find enumerated the various species of terrestrial and fluvial molluscs identified by me during the expedition to those mountains and neighbouring areas in June of last year. In perusing this document, you will at once note how this research conducted exclusively in small province of Sicily, albeit one of the most interesting, has expanded Sicilian malacology by the addition of several new species. By how many more could it be further enriched were the devotees of this science to investigate with equal zeal all other parts of this classical land of ours?

Terrestrial and fluvial malacology in Sicily has hitherto been neglected, since the study of zoology – you yourself have had occasion in the past to draw attention to this fact – has been inadequately cultivated among us; nor have those foreigners who have come to till our pastures been of any assistance in illuminating that branch of natural history, since during their fleeting visits they have contented themselves with describing only those species which have been presented to them, and have not shown any willingness to venture further into the island. Thus Deshayes, during his expedition to Morea, visited the east coast of the island but found few species to describe; Jan noted a few more in his *Catalogue*, attributing to them strange names; while the German Philippi, to say nothing of the others, listed only the most common species. It behoves the Sicilians themselves to undertake this task, and I am rash enough to hope that it will be carried to a speedy and successful conclusion now that in various parts of the island, in spite of the manifold difficulties, the science of Faunus is being cultivated, and with enthusiasm, and that following your own generous example, malacological objects will be identified and described.

In keeping with my wish to further this enterprise, as far as in me lies, I have begun by researching the Nebrodi Mountains. These mountains have never previously been visited by malacologists and ought on that account, and on account of the cosmic influences brought to bear on them, to have presented to me some interesting molluscs.

And indeed among the inaccessible crags of that mountain range, whose peaks rise some 5,000 feet above sea level, vast plains can be observed, the largest of which is some 1,000 acres in size and is called the Plain of the Battle, since it was here that the Normans engaged some 20,000 Saracens in one of the most bloody battles of the Middle Ages, ending with a Norman victory and the cruel extermination of the Saracen forces.

The springs are abundant and of varying temperatures, some providing irrigation as they snake through meadows enamelled with flowers, others furiously eating into the sides of the mountains as they rush downhill to give birth to the region's rivers.

There Nature displays all its glorious power; there the splendid oak, ash, elm, holm oak and cork tree cover the slopes of the mountains and the depths of the valleys, while holly, pine and maple stretch up to the ice-covered summits which, whether adorned with the beech or bare of all vegetation, split the secondary limestone; there every manner of tree and herb prospers, and together they spread the most delightful fragrance all around and offer the botanist ample material for his learned dissertations.

The variety of wildlife inhabiting those regions, in the caves, the woods, the waters, in the trunks of the decaying trees, in the cracks of the rocks or on the flowers, is prodigious; so that one is everywhere witness to a mysterious language, now expressed in yells and cries, now in melodies and laments, now in the buzz of the insects, now in the hiss of the snakes. This language, as eloquent as the language of love, resounds from the hollows in the rocks, and by filling the spirit with a sweet melancholy gives it focus, and by inviting it to lay aside every frivolity of human society elevates it to the idea of the sublime.

The whole of Sicily does not offer such a profusion and variety of objects, particularly for the attention of the botanist or the zoologist, as does the Madonie region in its entirety; nor is there any spot more suitable for the contemplation of the grandeur of nature, since I share Zimmerman's view that in solitude the faculties of the soul are rendered supremely alive, acute, expansive and sublime.

It would cause me much delight to expatiate more fully on the pleasing sensations the sight of the Madonie produced in me, if I did not fear to bore you by exceeding the permitted limits of a simple letter. However, I am unable to conceal from you that, in the midst of such delectable sensations, I felt arising from time to time in my spirit the regret that Sicily, however rich in every natural bounty, as yet possesses no account of either the fauna or the flora of the Nebrodi. For this latter, Sicily turns to our friend Filippo Perlatore as the one who, being already a distinguished student of Botany and having herborised in those mountains, can and must provide science with a work of value and interest. And it consoles me to hope that zoology will be enriched by you, who have already placed science in your debt and who in your work and your genius are following in the footsteps of your distinguished father.

APPENDIX TWO

Note on divers species of terrestrial and fluvial molluscs of Sicily. By Enrico Pirajno, Baron of Mandralisca. Extracted from the Literary Journal, *No. 230, 1842).*

Last year, while publishing the *Catalogue of the Molluscs of the Madonie*, I promised to write on the general terrestrial and fluvial malacology of Sicily. This was the purpose of my expedition into those mountains, and subsequently into the Caronie and into the countryside surrounding Messina, Catania, Syracuse and other places. To honour fully my promise to the public, I should be obliged to travel over the remainder of the island, to search out the molluscs resident in various places, to study and describe them, all of which will require much time and effort.

And while I will happily continue with this enterprise as that which will best serve as adornment to my country, and although my recent efforts have not been in vain, and indeed through them Sicilian malacology has extended its domain over many new species, or over ones believed not native to these parts, I have thought fit to publish at this moment the present note which will, I trust, appease at least in part the curiosity of the lovers of this science.

TWO

The Tree of the Four Oranges

The *San Cristofero* made its way into the port through a crush of boats, caiques and skiffs, each with fishermen plying the oars, attending to ropes, sails, lamps, nets, working with tallow, tow, tar; it proceeded through shouts, yells, cries bawled out inside individual boats, from boat to boat, from boat to quay where women and children stood huddled together adding to the din and commotion. A further crowd gathered at the Saracen houses above the harbour; windows, balconies, verandas, terraces, roofs, walls, battlements, rounded and pointed arches, haphazard breeches in the wall giving a glimpse of curtains, clothes, dresses, table-cloths and handkerchiefs blowing in the wind.

Above the hubbub, above the noisy, rowdy mass below on the quay and in the houses, there loomed by contrast, in all its calm majesty, the pink, living stone of the Rock, with its ammunition store, temple of Diana, water tanks and castle on the summit. And above the row of low houses, against the backcloth of the Rock, stood the two imposing towers of the Cathedral, single- and mullion-windowed, topped by pyramidal cusps, both were so suffused with the same pink light as to seem engendered by the Rock, wrenched from it and given separate life by earthquake or by the conscious, thousand-year labours of storm, wind, fresh-water rains or burning salt-water gales. The commotion concerned the huge catches landed in those days. There was no end of excited talk of kilo upon kilo of sardines, scombroids, horse-mackerel, anchovies, of blue fish in such profusion as to cause even the elders to wonder if those seas had ever before yielded up such bounty.

Excitement mounted, with quarrels between fleet and fleet,

crew and crew, races to arrive first and secure the best place on the sixty steps. And there was rivalry, near warfare, between family and family. After the shouting was done and the washing pulled into the houses, windows were slammed furiously shut. The panes glinted in the sun as it set on the horizon over the headland at Santa Lucia, in the direction of Imera, Solunto, l'Aspra, Monte Pellegrino. It was November, almost Martinmas, and the whole coast was still a shimmer of fish scales, glimmering like the gold stones in the mosaics in the Cathedral ceiling, or between the angels' peacock wings in the vaults, between the vine leaves and the palms on the crossbeams, and in the flowing locks of Christ Pantocrator.

Calm was restored. Little by little the quay emptied.

'Giovanni, we're in Cefalu!' exclaimed the Lipari merchant on board the *San Cristoforo*, as though awakening with a start from the spell cast over him by that riotous life-filled spectacle. He smiled and turned to the boy to receive from him too some sign of satisfaction. Instead, he found him depressed, in the grip of fear or ill-humour.

'Our fishermen in the Aeolian islands don't make such a racket. And everybody else manages to stay calm,' said Palamara, the young servant.

'But this is Sicily, Giovanni!' replied the merchant, putting his hand on the boy's shoulder. Giovanni looked at him, drew a deep breath and laughed uproariously.

'Come on. They're starting to disembark,' said the merchant. 'Let's go and get the chest.'

Giovanni looked down at the round, half-eaten roll in his hand which, in the excitement of entering port, he had forgotten to finish. He leaned over the railing of the quarterdeck and tossed it into the sea. A shoal of grey mullets instantly went for it, creating foam and spray on the surface of the water.

As soon as the gangway was in place, Chinnici and Bajona were the first on board. Whatever the explanation, those two guardians of the law managed to be present in every street, courtyard, alleyway, square, doorway, incline and descent along the entire shoreline. At any hour, from first light till three or four o'clock in the night. Taciturn, surly and suspicious, Chinnici was noted for

his permanently outstretched palm. Always the same, since the
day he had first set foot in Cefalu two years previously. He would
present himself at the grocer's with a list: pasta, tomato purée,
goat's cheese, sheep's cheese, cream cheese, tuna, roe, herrings,
stockfish... (you know how it is, wife and three children to support, each with an appetite that would shame a wolf). With his
thumb and index finger he would dip his hand into a waistcoat
pocket, draw out a silver piece, look the shopkeeper straight in
the eye, put the coin under his nose. 'Well now? How are you off
for change?' he would say. 'Your excellency enjoys a little joke,'
came the usual reply. 'How could I ever change that? You can
hand it in next time you pass by.' The same story with the
butcher, the fishmonger, the baker, the water-seller, the green-
grocer. He even took advantage of Ersilia, the old woman who
had her regular place on the street where, depending on the
season, she sold chicory, artichokes, asparagus, fennel, snails.

Bajona's little weakness – perhaps because he was a bachelor
and a Neapolitan into the bargain – was for anything in a skirt.
Crucilla, Francavilla, Marchifava, Giudecca and the whole of the
slum area were the districts he preferred. He would turn up at a
certain hour, belly protruding and moustache neatly trimmed,
white envelope in hand, knock at a door where the man of the
house was a guest of the Vicaria prison or else of Favignana.
'Who is it?' 'It's Bajona, the law, open up. I've news from your
husband.' Click click, and there he was inside.

They presented themselves to the captain shoulder to shoulder,
the one, Chinnici, as dark as a crow, the other, Bajona, tall and as
fair and red as a ripe peach.

'Cargo?'

'Liquid foam fire.'

'Talking bollocks, are we?'

'God forbid!'

'Well then?'

'Have a look for yourselves,' said the captain, pulling back the
hatch. The two leaned forward, shading their eyes to see more
clearly into the darkness. Bones? Salt? Flour? Manna? Snow? Or
perhaps some of that dust from Cyprus for ladies' cheeks and
hair?

Neither dared open his mouth.

'Can't see a fucking thing.' It was Bajona who spoke.

'Down below?' asked the captain.

'What do you mean? What are you saying?' said Bajona.

'You said...' began the captain.

'I said you can't see a thing...' said Bajona.

'Except something white...'

'A Virgin Mary!' interrupted the merchant, throwing open the side of the wooden chest Giovanni was cradling in his arms. In a niche, as though framed by the straw, there appeared the head of a woman, cut off at the base of the neck.

She was a beautiful woman, stately, well-nourished, her glance empty and distant, her neatly parted hair flowing back like the waves of the sea. On her head she wore a crown or hat in the form of a water vessel. The statue was of terracotta, slightly damaged, with one crack running across the left eye and another going from the bottom of the nose, cutting into the lip and ending on the chin. Other lesser cuts criss-crossed the forehead. Chinnici and Bajona stood transfixed staring in turn at the Madonna, at that man with the scoffing smile who had spoken, at the stolid, unmoving servant, at the group which had appeared on either side of them from nowhere.

'What Virgin Mary?' Bajona managed to stutter out.

'Kore,' rejoined the merchant.

'Saint Kore?' said Bajona.

'No. Just Kore,' said the merchant.

'Who are you? What do you want?' blurted Bajona.

'Nothing more than a passenger who wants to disembark. Let me introduce myself: Don Gaetano Profilo, thirty-three years old, native of Lipari, a merchant by trade. And this is my servant, Giovanni Palamara, seventeen years old, also a native of Lipari.' So saying, the merchant handed Bajona his papers. Bajona stared at them a moment, pretending to be able to read, then handed them over to Chinnici. Chinnici held them up under his nose, and with the aid of his index finger laboriously spelt out the words.

'Are you selling these Madonnas?' asked Bajona.

'No...' replied the merchant with a smile.

'Then what have you come to Cefalu to sell?'

'I am here to buy.'

'Buy what?'

'Tuna fish – pickled tuna, steaks, roe, heart, liver, entrails.'

'And this Madonna?'

'A present.'

'Who for?'

'For the Baron Mandralisca from the apothecary Carnevale, a friend of his who resides in Lipari.'

'What's he going to do with it? A Madonna head of the same clay as the vases they make – no offence intended – over at Santo Stefano Camastro, and all covered in cracks into the bargain… these nobles, they're weird folk,' pontificated Chinnici. The merchant, smiling at him, closed the chest.

'May we disembark?'

'All right,' said Bajona.

'All right,' said Chinnici.

The merchant, having said goodbye to the captain and the two policemen, set off with his servant, but stopped, turned back and said:

'The "liquid foam fire" the captain declared corresponds to pumice stone; and if in the future he talks of the "sweet tear of autumnal fluid", he means malvasia wine; and if he refers to "marine wall rosebuds", you can take it he's talking about capers.'

'Ah,' said Bajona.

'Ah,' said Chinnici.

'Our captain talks in metaphors, the language of people who live out their days going back and forth on the seas, like the Bedouins in the desert.'

'Ah,' said Bajona and Chinnici together.

The captain, none too pleased at this revelation, took out a piece of paper and handed it over.

Is it necessary to repeat that Bajona could not read and that it would have taken Chinnici a year to decipher the document?

So, entertaining a great respect for the reader and well aware that real time and narrative time are sometimes in conflict, we reproduce it here below.

Lipari, 8 November 1856

In the name of God and in the hope of salvation, I have in this harbour of Sotto Il Monastero loaded the deck and hold of this ship, the San Cristofero, against the account, and at the full liability of Signor Ferlazzo Onofrio. The Master, Bartolomeo Barbuto, is charged with transporting and delivering at the end of the voyage, in Cefalu, the below named and duly enumerated wares, in dry, whole and serviceable condition.

The aforementioned Captain pledges on his safe arrival to consign the said goods to Signor Michelangelo Di Paola, at which time the hire fee will be duly paid as per contract.

As sole proof of completion of the contract, this document, and any other relevant papers, will be signed by the Captain, and in the event of his not being able to write, will be signed by some other competent third party. All other documents shall be deemed null and void.

Item: 1428 (one thousand four hundred and twenty eight) chests of pumice stone.

Item: 175 (one hundred and seventy five) gallons of malvasia wine.

Item: 7 (seven) barrels of prime quality, salted capers.

Leaving Chinnici to expend untold energy on his reading, we will follow our merchant and his young companion Palamara, wooden chest over one shoulder and his master's personal effects clutched with his other arm against his side, all muscle and high spirits, walking with the lithe nimbleness of a man with two goldfinches perched on one finger.

Having walked down the quay, they passed through the Maritime Gate, and set off up the road known as Fiume. Giovanni found himself exhilarated and engrossed by the spectacle of the teeming street-life of the city: gangs of boys running everywhere, dashing out from alleyways, from squares, from streets with names like Della Corte, Porto Salvo, Vetrani, from courtyards, leaping up from warehouse basements, cavorting down stairs that appeared suddenly in the walls and wound upwards, towards the heavens, to end nowhere; old men standing in the doorways busily repairing coops and nets; arrogant women, huge baskets brimful of dripping clothes balanced on their heads, hands pressed firmly against sides, making their way back from the mouth of the underground river, the Cefalino, near the Pirajno and Martino houses, where the stones and basins had been in use for centuries as washing-place and bath-house. The cadenced ring of countless hammers falling on fresh leather, as unseen cobblers laboured in their workshops, resounded even over the myriad conversations, voices, shouts and guffaws.

The merchant, as he had when watching the earlier quayside spectacle from the decks of the *San Cristoforo*, looked everywhere, elated and smiling.

They passed the church of San Giorgio, the Orphanage, the church of Sant'Andrea, the monastery of the Hermit Fathers, and reached the corner of Strade Badia, a street as narrow and straight as a blade, running all the way from Strada Fiume to the square in front of the church. At the foot of the street the massive, soaring, left-hand bell tower of the Cathedral of the Most Holy Saviour (the Bishop's Tower, according to the experts) dominated the scene.

'Here we are,' said the merchant. 'Baron Mandralisca lives in this street.'

He asked a nun, encased in skirts, mantles and veils, standing in ecstasy in front of a tabernacle, where the palace was. Without raising her eyes from the naked, arrow-covered, bleeding body of Saint Sebastian, the nun pointed to a stoutly bolted door near by. The merchant lifted the cast-iron, lion-head door-knocker and delivered first a gentle blow on the door, then a series of blows which grew in volume and frequency. The women across the way stopped to stare at the two hapless foreign gentlemen and broke into a loud cackle. The merchant replied with a broad smile but did not ask for an explanation of the silence and deafness that reigned in that house. He came to a decision; he put his shoulder to the door, and it gave way like a damask curtain.

While the two were making their way up the stairs, a clatter of clogs announced the arrival of Rosario, the Baron's butler and manservant, red in the face, out of breath, shoes unlaced, striped apron pulled over his uniform.

'Jesus and Mary, Jesus and Mary!' he exclaimed as he came towards them. He came to a halt when he became aware that the two, quite unabashed, had no intention of stopping.

'Who are you? What do you want?'

The merchant, smiling, continued climbing the stairs, with Giovanni close behind. Rosario found himself almost face to face with them. Terrified, he stretched out his arms, which only had the effect of displaying his full girth.

'Stop! No further!' he intimated in a high-pitched, quivering voice. 'You can't go up there.'

'Announce me at once to Baron Mandralisca,' the merchant told him, placing an envelope in his hand.

'The Baron is resting... I mean, he's working... He's writing ... and when he's writing, he doesn't want...'

'Just announce me,' the merchant interrupted him.

'Yes sir,' said Rosario. He turned and, with his legs slightly akimbo, clambered heavily up the stairs.

The merchant and Giovanni quickly reached the landing and waited in the entrance. Giovanni set down the suitcase, and then, more gingerly, the chest.

'Welcome to this house, sir,' said Mandralisca, appearing at the doorway of his study, dressed in silk house-coat and skullcap, quill pen between his fingers, peering at them over a pince-nez balanced uncertainly on the tip of his nose.

'Giovanni Interdonato,' replied the counterfeit merchant, with a deep bow.

'The deputy?'

'If your Excellency still believes that there is a deputation...'

'No, no, you know that I am referring to 1848...we were colleagues, but I don't remember ever having met you in Parliament. Were you not in exile? In London, I seem to recall or in Paris.'

'I was and still am in Paris. Even now when you believe you see me here before you, in conversation with you,' added Interdonato in a low voice. 'I, sir, have the honour of being the merchant Gaetano Profilio from Lipari, charged with visiting your lordship by the apothecary Carnevale, who sends you this present,' – he pointed to the wooden chest on the floor – 'as a mark of respect and gratitude. For the rest, the card which preceded me should have explained clearly...'

'Yes, yes, I understand,' interrupted the Baron, smiling. He

put the pen down on a shelf and came towards him, hands outstretched. They greeted each other with a warm handshake.

'Please, make yourself at home, come into my study,' said the
Baron, putting his arm around the other's shoulder as though
intending to push him forward. Interdonato turned to indicate his
servant Palamara who, arms crossed on his chest and a smile fixed
on his features, stood there enjoying the whole scene.

'Ah yes, Rosario will take care of him,' said the Baron, pulling
a bell cord.

Rosario appeared immediately, elegant in his uniform but with
a look of evident displeasure on his face.

'Your excellency...'

'Fix up that boy in your quarters and bring the gentleman's
baggage to the Green Room which overlooks the terrace. Leave
the chest where it is,' ordered Mandralisca.

He went into the study with Interdonato, closing the door
behind him.

Such was the confusion and disorder induced by the relentless
search for truth that the Baron's chamber could have been the
studio of a Saint Jerome or Saint Augustine, or a cross between
the cell of the learned Sicilian monk Fazello and the laboratory of
Paracelsus. On all sides, lining the walls, stood cabinets filled
with books old and new, with codices, with parchments all overflowing and cascading, individually or in random piles, on to the
desk, the armchairs, the floor. On top of the cupboards there was
an array of stuffed birds from Sicily, Malta and the Aeolian
islands, perched in the most bizarre poses on stands or branches,
some with one foot, others with both, all complete with staring
glass eyes. Telescope and armillary sphere. Inside the display
cabinets and cases, on the surface of tables and consoles, the
greatest profusion of objects: marble heads, hands, feet and arms;
terracotta pieces, obols, lanterns, tiny pyramids, spindles, masks,
ancient pots and stone bowls, both intact and cracked; shells from
snails and sea-creatures. In the few remaining spaces on the walls,
diplomas and canvases. Facing the desk, in the space between the
cabinets, hung Antonello's portrait of the Unknown Man; on the
wall opposite, above the desk, pride of place was occupied by an
enlarged and coloured copy, executed by the painter Bevelacqua

to a commission from the Baron himself, of Passafiume's seventeenth-century map of Cefalu. The city was viewed from above, from the perspective of a hovering bird, with the walls shutting it off from the sea and the banners fluttering from the ramparts at the four gates. The little houses, all identical, all packed together like lambs in the pen formed by the semicircle of the walls sloping down to the sea and the Rock closing the city off from the rear, were cut into neat, square blocks by the transverse line of Strada Regale and the vertical lines of the streets that ran from the mountain down to the sea. Like huge protective shepherds, the Cathedral and the Bishop's Palace, the Dominican Convent, the Abbey of Saint Catherine, the Grand Hostelry loomed over the flock of the houses. In the gale-lashed harbour, galleys, feluccas and brigs tossed on the waves. A scroll with the legend CEPHALEDU SICILIAE URBS PLACENTISSIMA was deployed like an oriflamme or flying jib in undulating folds in the sky, and above it was the oval coat of arms, edged with coils and whorls, divided into two sections, of which the upper panel depicted King Ruggero offering to God his Saviour the model of the Cathedral and the lower panel displayed three grey mullets in a star formation, biting simultaneously into a loaf of bread.

For Interdonato, that coat of arms recalled the bread tossed into the water by Giovanni and immediately devoured by the grey mullets. His mind was filled with flashes of thought, images, fantasies. The three diverging tails or legs representing the coat of arms of Cefalu, and of all Sicily, but equally representing a universal coat of arms of this globe called Earth, a symbol of history since the emergence of humanity until the present: the struggle for bread, a bestial struggle where the strong prevail and the weak succumb... (*Qu'est-ce que la propriété?*)... But today is the vigil of the Great Reform: the mullet, *cefalo* in the Sicilian tongue... every mullet will be allotted an equal place and the loaf divided in equal parts, with no more killing, no more animal-like savagery. And *cefalo* like *Cefalu* means head, and head implies reason, mind, man... might it be that from this stretch of land...?

He smiled and took his eye off the map, saying to Mandralisca: 'Never seen such a display of science, not even in Paris in the

home of Victor Hugo, the writer, nor in the residence of Proudhon, the philosopher.'

'Please, for goodness' sake...' the Baron warded off the compliment from a mixture of embarrassment and surprise at hearing
such names. He moved the books off a chair to let his guest sit
down.

'I am only now getting down to the work on the general terrestrial and fluvial malacology of Sicily which has been absorbing
my energies for some time, and which, I may say, has left me
thoroughly worn out,' explained Mandralisca, collapsing onto a
seat behind the desk as though exhausted.

'And do you really believe, Mandralisca, that at this moment in
history there are people out there waiting with baited breath to
find out the private facts of life and the intimate details of the trails
and shells of Sicilian slugs?'

'No, no, I'm not saying...' countered Mandralisca, slightly
offended. 'It's just that I promised, was it fifteen years ago? when
I published my monograph on the malacology of the Madonie
mountains...'

'My dear Mandralisca, don't you realise what has been going
on in those fifteen years? Aren't you aware of the times we are
living through?'

'How dare you?' Mandralisca spluttered.

'Ah but I do dare, Baron, because you are no *crazy fool*, no
imbecile or feeble minded buffoon, unlike the majority of Sicilian
nobles or scholars. You are a man gifted with the capacity of
mind and heart to understand. And you are one of the few who
has never reneged.'

'So you, you...' Mandralisca made a futile effort to get the
words out, opening his eyes wide behind the lenses of his pince-
nez, switching his glance rapidly from Interdonato's face to the
face above him, on Antonello's portrait. Those two faces, the one
alive and the other in paint, were identical: the same olive colour-
ing of the skin, the same sharp and searching eyes, the same
pointed nose, and above all the same ironic, piercing smile.

'The mariner!' exclaimed Mandralisca.

'Yes, Baron, I was the mariner on the sailing ship which four
years ago travelled from Lipari to Cefalu, via the port of Tindaro.

And I knew perfectly well what you were hugging close to your breast, wrapped up in that waxed canvas.'

'How?'

'Catena.'

'Carnevale's daughter?'

'Yes sir.'

'A rather unconventional young lady.'

'Catena is my fiancée.'

'I beg your pardon.'

'No need. Her unconventionality consists in her having seen her fiancé, in person, on no more than five occasions, always fleetingly and always in hiding. And her ordeal was sharpened by the presence, an elusive and evanescent but also perpetual and enraging presence of this portrait by Antonello which, as you yourself pointed out, could not have been a better resemblance of me if I had been the sitter. The smile was the final straw. Now you see why one day Catena deliberately ripped the mouth, and why the apothecary her father sold it? The poor girl had the misfortune to fall in love with a revolutionary.'

'But what were you doing on that ship disguised as a sailor?'

'I was making my way from Paris, Baron, where I had been charged by the Executive Committee, by Landi, Friscia, Michele Amari, Carini and Milo Gugino, to keep in touch with Mazzini and the National Committee in London and with other groups of exiles scattered all over the world, in Marseilles, Genoa, Turin, Florence, Pisa, Livorno, Tunis and Malta, not to mention Alexandria and Constantinople. I was, and still am, a kind of clandestine ambassador, always on the move, assuming the role of mariner or merchant or of some other poor devil so as to keep one step ahead of the police or, even worse, of spies and informers. So, when I had the good fortune to meet up with you, I was on the way from Livorno to the Aeolian islands to spend a few moments with Catena. From Palermo I proceeded to Tunis...'

، 'And now, Interdonato?' asked Mandralisca, growing more amazed by the minute.

'Now, Baron, time is short, these are explosive days. We are on the very eve of the Great Event. We have reached an agreement to act under a neutral banner, as you may have read in the

Free Word, all of us, Pisacane, Mordini, Pilo, Mazzini, Fabrizi, La Masa, Calvino, Errante...'

'What about La Farina?' asked Mandralisca timidly.

'That traitor, Cavour's lackey!' Interdonato exploded. 'Forgive me. My only regret is that he comes from Messina, like me ...and like Antonello,' he added with a smile. He paused, folded his arms, drew himself up straight, looked at the Baron unflinchingly and spoke in a clear voice. 'Baron, this time I came deliberately to your house to ask three favours of you.'

'Name them,' said the Baron, opening his arms, half willing and half hesitant.

'First: to hold here, in a house which is free of all suspicion, a meeting with the brothers in this district. I want to meet the two Bottas, Guarnera, Bentivegna, Civello, Buonafede, Gugino...'

'Poor Spinuzza...'

'I know, I know that he has been in jail for three years...but not for much longer, I promise.'

'The second?'

'To receive from your lordship a letter of introduction for Landolina in Syracuse. From there I will set sail for Malta.'

'Finally?'

'To leave with you, for a brief period, the boy you saw just now in the entrance hall. He's not my servant but the son of Palamara, a rich merchant in Lipari, Catena Carnevale's cousin. It was she who gave him his education. He's only seventeen and he's already aflame with revolutionary ideas. In Lipari, they were liable to seize him at any moment and lock him up in a cell in the castle above the citadel.'

Mandralisca began to drum with his fingers on the surface of his desk, absentmindedly, lost in thought. Interdonato watched him in amusement.

'Agreed,' said Mandralisca, awakening from his reverie with a start, and looking Interdonato full in the face. 'I will do my best to meet your requests, but I have to confess that the first will be the most difficult. Don't consider me cowardly or inhospitable. You have no idea how this house swarms with gossiping, empty-headed busybodies and, even more worrying, with devoted admirers of the Bourbon king. Don't lay the blame at my door. You must be aware how hard it is in Sicily to steer clear of so-called friends. You can defend yourself for a certain time, but then out of sheer weariness you give way, you surrender... And these people turn up at your door at any hour of the day or night with the most banal of excuses, which they present as the most pressing, urgent of problems. The truth of the matter is that they are terrified of being on their own, they are weighed down by the panic of existence. They couldn't give a damn for anything or anybody apart from themselves, because their deepest conviction is that the blessed state in which they alone were born was due to the irreversible will of God. As you were coming in you saw how Rosario, doing violence to a naturally peaceable and pliant temperament, has transformed himself into my personal gendarme... at least during those hours when I must work... Rather – I was wondering if it would not be better to meet with you and the others in an outhouse on one of my estates, Campo di Musa, not too far from Cefalu?'

There was a knock at the door and the butler entered to announce that the Baroness and Signorina Anna were already dressed for dinner.

'We can talk further another time,' said the Baron rising to his feet. He told Rosario: 'Accompany the gentleman to his room.'

The steam was rising from the pasta with its sauce of sardines, pine nuts, fennel and raisins, encouraging Interdonato, fork in hand, eyes half closed, to open his nostrils and abandon himself, after enduring so much hardship, to the pleasures of delicious, homely scents.

Annetta Parisi e Pereira, the Baron's niece, looked furtively at their guest and laughed with that tinkling laugh of hers. The talk turned to Parisian sauces, to couscous and the spices of Tunis and Malta, to the colourless cuisine – nothing but raw or boiled beef with, as occasional touch of fantasy, a side plate of beans – of Turin.

'Peasants and bumpkins!' pontificated Annetta.

'And those wines of theirs!' added Mandralisca. 'Sad and life-less, and as dull as the Turinese themselves.'

And they discussed fish: the cuttlefish, lobsters and squid of the Aeolian islands; the sardines, anchovies, horse mackerel from the seas around Palermo; the swordfish and saury pike from the Straits of Messina.

'Stuffed squid!' exclaimed Annetta, and immediately broke into a raucous guffaw such as was scarcely fitting for a young lady like her.

'Annetta!' her aunt called her to account.

'I'm sorry, very sorry,' said Annetta, trying to hold back her laughter. And she explained how when she was still living in the Aeolians that nickname had been attached (and it had been Catena who had invented it, Catena Carnevale herself) to a young lad who had been making eyes at her.

'Have you ever seen squid stuffed with breadcrumbs, eggs and cheese, drenched in its own ink? When you put it on the platter it's all firm and round, and shiny and smooth so that you think it's going to explode. That was just like Bartolo Cincotta. His father was a doctor. He had a squeaky little voice... The last I heard of him he was locked away in a seminary.'

'Some day he will make a fine bishop or even a cardinal,' smiled Interdonato.

'Oh that Catena... what an imagination she had!' said Annetta.

'She hasn't lost it, not at all,' said Interdonato. 'Quite the reverse. I believe it's now being given even freer rein.'

'In what way?'

'She's writing poetry.'

'Love poems, I bet.'

'Far from it. I would call them poems of hatred.'

'Hatred for whom?'

'For all that is perverted, unjust, inhuman in this world. She writes with special feeling about the pain and suffering of the fishermen, peasants, pumice-stone quarrymen of the Aeolians, about those sacred rights of theirs which have always been trampled on; she rails with the rage of the Furies against those who are responsible for the inequalities and afflictions...'

'Goodness!' exclaimed Annetta. 'Now that I think about it, I remember that she was always reading... or else embroidering.'

'She has certainly never stopped reading. I doubt if there is a single writer she is not familiar with. First she had a great passion for Italian writers, for Campanella, Bruno, Vico, Pagano, Filangieri... but now she's more drawn to the French, to Rousseau, Babeuf, Fourier, Proudhon as well as to Victor Hugo and Georges Sand. She never stops asking me to send her books from Paris. As for the embroidery, she says it helps relieve tension and at the same time it enables her to get to grips with what she has been reading.'

'Beccafichi!' shouted Rosalia, Rosario's wife, bursting into the dining room, serving dish in hand. Her dark, youthful, solid figure was the picture of joy and happiness.

'They must be eaten hot, piping hot,' she said, laying the stuffed sardines on the table.

'What's become of Giovanni, the young lad I entrusted to your care?' Mandralisca asked Rosalia.

'He was dying of starvation. Never seen a lad bolt his food so fast!' answered Rosalia, hands flailing in the air and coal-black eyes open wide.

'As fast as Rosario,' Mandralisca hazarded, with a smile.

'Oh, what's your Excellency saying? Rosario's got no appetite at all. He picks at everything. He suffers from acidity... nothing like Giovanni at all. This Giovanni's just a young lad... robust, good-looking, God bless him, he enjoys his food...'

'Come on, admit it. You're falling in love with him, Rosalia,' said Mandralisca, amused.

'Enrico!' his wife reproved him sternly.

'Mother of God, Excellency, what are you saying? He's just a boy, I could be his mother.'

'Rosalia, get back to the kitchen,' ordered the Baroness. Annetta burst into one of her full-throated laughs.

'Excuse me,' Interdonato said to Rosalia before she left. 'When the lad has finally finished eating, tell him, if the Baron and Baroness have no objection, to come in here.'

'Of course, of course,' said the Baron.

'As you wish,' said Rosalia graciously.

As they were about to proceed to the fruit and sorbets, they saw Giovanni Palamara emerge into the bright light of the dining-room, a smile on his face but eyes betraying embarrassment.

'Oh!' exclaimed Annetta. 'Good-looking as well! Rosalia got it right this time.'

Her aunt threw her a disapproving glance.

'Giovanni, what's this? Aren't you going to greet our hosts?' Interdonato asked him. Giovanni immediately bowed, but no one grasped what he murmured under his breath.

Annetta fired a barrage of questions at him, about his relatives and relatives' relatives, his friends and acquaintances, about the people of Lipari and Canneto, Santa Marina and Malfa di Salina, about all the towns in the seven islands of the tiny Aeolian archipelago. Giovanni replied in monosyllables, peevishly, intimidated by the familiarity assumed by that patrician Signorina.

'Giovanni,' said Interdonato when Annetta appeared to have finally run out of questions, 'if the Baron doesn't mind, would you go down to the entrance hall and bring up the chest. You are the only one who knows how to carry it.'

'At once,' said Giovanni, relieved at being able to free himself from the conversation with the young lady, and from the burden of having all eyes on him.

He returned with the chest, and placed it gently on the floor.

Interdonato rose to his feet, went over to the box, and with Giovanni's help drew out from the wood and straw an ancient terracotta Kore figure. He took it in both hands and placed it cautiously on a sideboard.

'Oh,' Mandralisca, the Baroness and their niece Annetta exclaimed simultaneously. Mandralisca began to tremble uncontrollably. Unable to remain seated, he rose to his feet, put his pince-nez in place and approached the Kore. He examined it in a state of ecstasy, his nose almost touching the top of the statue, running his eye over every segment, from head to neck, and then to the back where the wavy hair was gathered up in a chignon.

'Beautiful,' he exclaimed, 'beautiful beyond words. How can I thank the apothecary? Look,' he said, walking backwards but keeping his eyes fixed on the Kore, 'if I had to produce an image of the new Italy, Free and United, I would think of a statue like this...'

'Ah, too beautiful, Baron, too perfect... perhaps I should say too ideal,' said Interdonato. 'But there's another present, for

Annetta from Catena.' Interdonato put his hand inside the hollow in the crown on the statue's head and pulled out a little embroidered silk table-cloth. He opened it out and presented it to Annetta. She received it with evident delight and spread it out on the table to examine it more closely. Curiosity got the better even of the Baroness Maria Francesca and she too approached the table. At first view, it appeared an odd piece of work, sewn fancifully and without discipline. The borders consisted of drawn threads, but the needlework at the centre was a riot of the most disparate stitches: the moss stitch was confused with the cross stitch, which slid into the feather stitch and merged with the chain stitch. And the colours! It passed instantly from the most subtle, delicate shades to the most gaudy greens and fiery reds. It looks, thought the Baroness, like a tablecloth sewn by a madwoman possessed by a fury, who deliberately set aside laws, numbers, measure and harmony so as to make it seem that reason had deserted her. Nevertheless it was clear that the intricate needlework at the centre represented a tree with a knotty, twisted trunk, topped by a single leafless branch on one side, while the other was adorned by a green triangular patch of foliage and by lesser, extravagant marks. Four red balls, intended to look like oranges, hung from the branches over towards the right, with some words embroidered around them, in a semicircle, written backwards.

'It seems to be an orange tree. But what do those words mean?' asked Annetta.

'From where you are looking at it, it is indeed an orange tree,' replied Interdonato, still enjoying himself. 'But if you turn it over...'

'But it's Italy!' exclaimed Annetta, looking at the tablecloth from the other side.

'Yes, it's Italy,' confirmed Interdonato. 'And the four oranges become the four volcanoes of the Kingdom of the Two Sicilies – Vesuvius, Etna, Stromboli and Vulcano. And it is from here, suggests Catena, from these mouths of fire which have lain so long suppressed, and above all from Sicily which contains three in such a small area, that the flames of revolution will burst forth and set all Italy alight.'

APPENDIX ONE

Francesco Guardione: The Political Uprising in Cefalu in 1856. *Lecture delivered on 25 November 1906, in Cefalu, in the Church of Our Lady of Mercy, before the monument erected to Salvatore Spinuzza. Salvatore Gussio publisher, Cefalu, 1907.*

[...]

The year 1856 is remembered as the year of the Congress of Paris but is also memorable for the events which occurred in the south of Italy and for the initiatives taken that year in Sicily; having rejected the purely regionalist instincts which, however unworthy of a ruling aristocracy, had held sway until 1848, Sicily aspired now to a genuinely Italian nationalism, to the union of the various peoples, and to that liberty which was to be its beacon and lead it forth from darkest night. Palermo had its own central revolutionary committee, which was in correspondence with the most eager spirits in the interior of the island and which drew comfort from the words of those exiles who, gathered in lands where freedom reigned, continually harried the Bourbon dynasty, affording it no peace, making it unsure of itself and driving it to acts of terrible vengeance against rebels who were already restive and prepared to resort to violence against the forces of an absolutist regime that would gladly have chained up thought itself!

The evening of 23 November the Lieutenant-General Paolo Ruffo, Prince of Castelcicala, received word of the rising in Mezzojuso the previous evening. On the 16 November, Francesco Bentivegna had gone to Palermo and to certain other towns and had, in discussion with the conspirators, chosen the 12 January 1857, a heroic date associated with glorious deeds, for the insurrection. However, Bentivegna altered this decision on his own initiative, and on 22 November descended on Mazzojuso at the head of three hundred armed men, unfurled the tricolour and to the cry of 'Viva l'Italia' proceeded to Villafrate, Vicari, Ciminna and Ventimiglia.

On the 24th of the same month, the Bourbon army under the command of Ghio entered Mazzojuso, causing the rebels to disperse and leaving Bentivegna to wander alone in the countryside, hiding from the murderous weaponry of adversaries who would never have succeeded in taking him had they not been aided by the treachery of his hosts.

More serious and solemn events unfolded at Cefalu where the preparations, always hazardous and risky, had been completed in the mysterious night hours in the house of the Botta family. To this house, heedless of the prevailing climate of fear, the conspirators made their way fearlessly and frankly, and from it a ray of light was to spread over the land. There, the few were responsive to the call of grand deeds; there the flag of Italy, destined to fly high and inspire sacred sentiments, was prepared. In the Botta family house, that fellowship of intrepid souls, united for the purpose of defying tyranny, awaited the command which was to be communicated by an emissary. It arrived after sunset, at 2200 hours, on 25 November, and the people of Cefalu were inflamed by the call to revolution. But Palermo – Palermo remained passive, its much-vaunted Committee thus leaving only a faintly comic memory of its doings.

Elisabetta and Giuseppina Botta unfurled over their own home, the focus of the conspiracy, the banner they had sewn with their own hands. The coming and going of the conspirators, each armed with his own weapons, was constant; Salvatore Guarnera, Nicolo Botta, Andrea Maggio, Vincenzo Spinuzza and Pasquale Maggio all turned up at the Botta household; but neither Carlo Botta, who had been dispatched to Gratteri to have the forces there link up with the revolution, nor Alessandro Guarnera were present. The latter was in Gratteri on the day of the 25th, and, having learned of the rising only in the evening, returned at once to Cefalu. The revolutionaries boldly paraded through the city, some besieging the police station, capturing it and disarming the agents without causing injury, while Nicolo Botto, Pasquale and Andrea Maggio, with the aid of others of the rebel forces, moved off in two squadrons; the first headed by Andrea Maggio attacked the city guards, while the other under Nicolo Botta proceeded to the prison situated below the City Chambers, released Salvatore Spinuzza, proclaimed him leader of the revolution and set up a provisional government. Nor was the popular frenzy satisfied by these gestures, for the following day new detachments, notably those from Campofelice headed by the lawyer Cesare Civello, reinforced the revolution and even bolder acts were executed: the official papers of the Sub-prefecture were put to the flame.

Meanwhile, during the night of the 25 to 26 November, Carlo Botta, on a mission to various towns in the vicinity to inform them of the plans for the uprising, heard word of the outbreak of revolution in Cefalu and, having conferred with Francesco Buonafede, returned immediately to Campofelice to hold further discussions with the Termini Imerese committee; when that mission was completed, he made his way back to Cefalu, a town still in the grip of insurrectionary fervour. He met up with Civello's men, the various detachments merged and entered Cefalu together on the morning of the 26th. The seventeen-year-old Giovanni Palamara, a member of the Civello detachment, was elected standard-bearer. A squadron headed by Francesco Buonafede marched from Gratteri and reached Cefalu on 27 November, only to be turned back to reinforce the revolt elsewhere.

News of the rebellion was conveyed hourly to Palermo; Castelcicala, the Prince Lieutenant, dispatched a heavily armed frigate, the *Sannio* which, when it appeared offshore, was greeted by the national banner fluttering from the battlements of Cefalu harbour. The disembarkation of the military was met with lively resistance, and if the rising was put down that day, the 27 November, by the sheer deployment of over-whelming force, there is no gainsaying the damage done to the revolutionary cause by the clerics in the nearby seminary. On the appearance of the royal frigate, these latter fled Cefalu and dispersed to their home villages bringing news of the most recent developments, thereby heading off uprisings in the surrounding towns, and dissuading the already-formed squadrons from joining the revolutionary forces. The rebels strove mightily to prevent the soldiers from landing, but in the face of the threats, issued in keeping with routine royal practice, to bombard the city, devotion to their native place caused them to submit and flee from Cefalu. The intention was to continue the struggle in the neighbouring mountains, where there was no shortage of communities willing to co-operate in this noble enterprise, and indeed on the road they encountered contingents from Gratteri, Collesano and Castelbuono marching, with all the boldness of victorious phalanxes, on Cefalu.

After much aimless wandering, at sunset on the 28th the combatants divided into small groups to seek shelter. Nicolo and Carlo Botta, Salvatore Spinuzza and Francesco Buonafede, who was familiar with the locality, found a hut near Gratteri where they remained in hiding for several days. In these desolate, terrifying localities, they received a great deal of support and assistance from various quarters; the people of Gratteri displayed generous sentiments, and the Sidele family in particular distinguished themselves for their nobility of action.

The government instituted a reign of terror against the population, and, now that all hope had been crushed, life resumed its previous grimness. The leaders of the revolutionary movement were reputed to be Spinuzza, the brothers Nicolo and Carlo Botta, Andrea Maggio and Alessandro Guarnera, and to facilitate their arrest the government put a price on their head. With the arrest of the families of the fugitives, they showed themselves prepared to stoop to any form of barbarity. Nowhere was this more evident than in the treatment, an outrage to standards of civilisation or humanity, of Elisabette and Giuseppina Botta and of their mother, Signora Concetta; the three ladies were arrested, held in a dreadful, fetid jail together with common criminals for a period of several months and then transported to the prison in Palermo.

The five reputed leaders of the movement were endlessly harried and forced to keep on the move but, with the faith of martyrs, they swore a solemn oath that, if captured, they would endure any form of torture sooner than reveal the names of their comrades. And indeed, later on, none of those lips opened to pronounce a cowardly word. Little more than a month after the rebellion, the five fugitives were escorted from San Mauro to the house of Mauro Giallolombardo, cousin of the Botta brothers, in Pettineo; the two responsible for this high-minded deed were the priest Zito and Rosaria Calascibetta. Lodged in a house belonging to Giovanni Sirena, they turned their minds to finding the most effective means of escaping into exile in Malta. No other possibility appeared viable since each day brought news of fresh arrests, of Giuseppe Maggio, of Pasquale and Andrea Maggio, sons of the late Antonino, of Giuseppe Re who gave himself up, of Salvatore Bevilacqua, Antonino Spinuzza, Salvatore Maranto and of the Cefalu peasant Santi. The sufferings of all were great, nor was there any grounds for hope of release or reduction of sentence.

The most painstaking investigations were underway all over Sicily to trace the whereabouts of the five fugitives; this tireless but fruitless task was entrusted to Gambaro, to Bajona and Chinnici, who spared themselves no effort in their eagerness to capture the leaders of the Cefalu revolt.

Captain Gambaro's efforts were in vain, and he found himself facing threats of dismissal for manifest incompetence. Bajona and Chinnici, police agents, were summoned to strengthen the investigation and they, in a comparatively brief time, discovered that the fugitives were in Patti, sheltering in the home of a comrade, Raimondo Dixitdomini.

Chinnici went with all haste to Patti, took possession of Dixitdomini's house, subjected him to various forms of ill treatment without, however, managing to wring the secret from him. Bajona showed no less zeal than his confrère, and the extremes of ill fortune willed that a letter entrusted to the mariner Gerbino fell into his hands. Nicolo Botta had given him the task of withdrawing a sum of money left by the family in the keeping of the priest Restivo [...]. Bajona then resorted to every device in the police armoury; he summoned to Pettineo no less than three hundred men, caught up with Gerbino in Finale, dragged him into a nearby hotel and brutally extorted from him the secret of the place where the wanted men were in hiding.

Gerbino was then forced to accompany Bajona and Chinnici to Pettineo, and there at nightfall on the 5 February, with the assistance of seven fellow agents, of the Mayor and the City Guard, they seized Sirena, who was responsible for concealing the five fugitives and for handing the letter to Gerbino. Gerbino then showed them the house where Salvatore Spinuzza, Nicolo and Carlo Botta, Alessandro Guarnera and Andrea Maggio, the leaders of the Cefalu uprising, were hiding. That night the residence was surrounded by a large force, and at dawn came the order to launch the attack: the sounds of the roll of drums and of the tolling of monastery bells, which rang out to give the alarm and summon aid, mingled with the din of the assault, which was itself terrifying. Four of the police company attacked the building, but were repulsed with two of the assault force sustaining injuries. Other reinforcements were brought up [...] and all engaged in pitched battle against the five. For nine and a half hours, the battle raged; there can be few other instances of such heroic resistance, which ended only when the ammunition was exhausted. Compelled to lay down their arms, Spinuzza, Nicolo and Carlo Botta, Guarnera and Maggio surrendered. The public forces, rather than applauding such valour, celebrated the event as a triumph!

On the 20 December 1856, following the unanimous decision of the Council of War in Palermo, which had the previous day passed sentence of death on him, Bentivegna was executed.

Everyone must be aware of the barbarous procedures and decision of the Supreme Court of Justice: it is sufficient for us to record the hypocritical words of the Marshal in Chief, Raffaele Zola, addressed to the Director General of Police. He wrote: 'I have the honour to assure you that all necessary measures have been taken to transport Signor Bentivegna to Mezzojuso, as have all arrangements required for the execution of the sentence. I have determined that the comforts of Holy Religion will be administered at three o'clock.' On the 22 December, the same Council of War condemned Salvatore Guarnera to death for having taken part in a subversive armed gang in Cefalu on the 25, 26 and 27 of November; the sentence was suspended to allow for a royal pardon, which was granted and the sentence commuted to one of 18 years in irons.

After these events, the city of Cefalu saw its houses deserted and desolate. Nicolosi, the Vice-Prefect, to appease his own desire for vengeance at not having the fugitive leaders of the revolution in his power, pursued a policy of arrest and persecution of persons of every class. He gave every sign of satisfaction when he learned of the arrest and impending trial of the five. The Council of War, in its formal meeting immediately after attendance at the mass of the Holy Spirit, formulated the following charges: 'All five are accused of high treason, and specifically of having conspired against His Majesty's Government and of having instigated his subjects to take up arms against the royal authority in Cefalu and places adjacent thereto; by mobbing and rioting, by the flying of a tricolour standard, by the beating of drums; by defacing royal emblems and images of our dearly beloved king and queen; by pillaging royal dispatch boxes and pulling down telegraph lines; by sequestering the royal couriers and violating the royal mail; by arresting royal officials; by disarming the forces of law; by placing a rebellious banner on the battlements of the port of Cefalu within sight of the royal steamship as it entered the harbour; by the devastation, sack and arson of the offices and palace of the Vice-Prefect of Cefalu, causing documents and registers to be burnt or destroyed; by the theft of two quintals and sixty-nine barrels of powder used by the road-building department for explosions to remove rocks; and lastly, by showing resistance to the forces of law, firing continually for nine and a half hours in Pettineo, in the province of Messina.'[1]

And with these charges, which must command a chapter in any history of the Risorgimento, he reaffirmed that the political uprising in Cefalu demonstrated a level of valour which prefigured the great deeds accomplished during the struggle for national unity. And, unanimously, finding that Salvatore Spinuzza, Nicolo and Carlo Botta, Alessandro Guarnera and Andrea Maggio, son of the late Ignazio, were guilty of the misdeeds mentioned above, confirmed the sentence of death on Salvatore Spinuzza, 25 years old, the same sentence with torture of the second degree for Nicolo Botta, 22 years old, for Carlo Botta, 19 years old, for Alessandro Guarnera, 26 years old, and for Andrew Maggio, 28 years old.

Sentence was handed down on the 11 March 1857, and three days later Salvatore Spinuzza was executed. His native city of Cefalu, which saw one of its best loved sons die before a firing squad, was shrouded in mourning. The citizenry drew together in silent pain, awaiting the great vengeance which would come with national redemption and with the removal of the scourge of the House of Bourbon, already condemned by the people. Nicolo and Carlo Botta, Alessandro Guarnera and Andrea Maggio were spared the firing squad, a pardon having been sought by the Council of War, but the commuted sentence of 18 years in irons condemned them to burial alive in the dungeons of Favignana.

[1] State Archive, Palermo, Police Papers, 1857.

APPENDIX TWO, OR INTERMEZZO

From The Diary of One of Garibaldi's Thousand, *by G.C. Abba*

On board the Lombardo, 1 May. Morning.
Sicily! Sicily! Something cloudy appeared in the blue haze between sea and sky; it was the sacred island itself!

Marsala, 11 May.

Suddenly a cannon shot is heard. What is it? 'Only a greeting,' said

Colonel Carini smiling. He was wearing a red tunic, with a great, broad-brimmed, plumed hat on his head. At the second shot, a huge cannon-ball passed us by with a roar, thudding between us and the Seventh Company, throwing up sand in its wake.

Marsala, 11 May, 3 a.m.

Last night at ten o'clock, Corporal Plona made me stand guard at the foot of a cliff, the last sentinel in our line. He left me there for five hours. I wrote verses to the stars.

Wednesday. During the 'Great Halt'.

There was a delightful scent in the air: but that field outside the walls of Marsala, strewn with blackish boulders and with those yellow flowers covering some stretches, began to fill me with a sense of dead things. Bixio passed by on horseback...

After him, followed some of the scouts who had been on the *Lombardo*, fine horses, fine horsemen, light-coloured uniforms...

Nullo came prancing along, an odd figure, totally relaxed on his mount; the torso of a Perseus, aquiline nose, the most handsome man on the expedition...

Missori from Milan, clad in a short tunic which heightens the impression he gives of being a grand lord, has a gracious red, gold braided cap on his head...

The others all in their salad days: the beguiling Manci from Trento calls to mind Grossi's Fiorina, so endowed is he with the air of an innocent maiden...

Finally Garibaldi himself arrived with the General Staff. Mounted on a bay horse fit for a Grand Vizier, he was seated in a splendid saddle with stirrups of the finest filigree work. He wore a red shirt and grey trousers, with a Hungarian style hat on his head and a silk handkerchief around his neck.

From the Estate of Rampagallo. Evening.

The sun poured down on us like liquid as we passed through the interminable undulating moorland, where grass grows and dies as in a cemetery. And never a spring of water, never a stream, never the outline of a village on the horizon. 'Where is this supposed to be, the Pampas?' exclaimed Pagani, who had been in America in his youth.

As we passed by, one of them said: 'Did you ever see desert like that one today? You could say we're here to help the Sicilians liberate their land from idleness!'

13 May. Salemi. From a monastery balcony, facing the glory of the sun.

A woman with a black cloth over her face stretched out her hand muttering something.
'What is it?' I asked.
'I am dying of hunger, your Excellency!'
'Are they trying to make fools of us here?' I exclaimed.

Salemi 14 May.

The General has assumed the dictatorship in the name of Italy and of Victor Emmanuel. The matter is discussed everywhere, and there is some dissatisfaction.

Salemi 15 May, 5 a.m.

The reveille is sounded. And Simonetta comes to tell us that we are off. A great young man, Simonetta. He cares nothing for himself, he lives only for other people. Is there guard duty to be done? Simonetta will come forward. A demanding service? There he is, frail and kind-hearted. Bread being shared out? He is the last in the queue to collect his share. He left his widowed father alone in Milan.
In a few minutes we're on the move.
The enemy is indeed a mere nine miles away. For two days and nights we have rested on this plateau among this poor, uncouth people. Who knows where we will sleep tonight? The artillery wagons are at the ready. The muzzle of the culverin stretches out. The artillery corps, almost all engineers, has been formed.

15 May, 11 a.m. On the hills of Pianto Romano.

There, over there, is the enemy! The mountain opposite is swarming with them; there must be some five thousand men. Our detachments have been lined up. The General is observing the enemy's movements from that point.
Colonel Carini's horse reared and threw him. It does not matter. He is immediately back in the saddle. I saw La Masa fall ahead of me; he must have hurt himself. I felt as though I had struck my own head against those rocks.

16 May. From the San Vito Monastery above Calatafimi.

Our companies came down at a brisk pace, singing.
At a bend in the road, Garibaldi on his horse loomed grandly over us

against the sky. It was a sky of glory from which a warm light poured down on us to blend with the scents of the valley and leave us all intoxicated.

Meantime the inhabitants of the village of Vita were fleeing, carrying with them their household goods, dragging their old folk and children. It was a heart-rending spectacle. We were saddened as we crossed the village and those poor folk stared at us, made gestures of compassion and said to us: 'Poor things!'

'What? Red trousers? Are the French already lining up with the Neapolitans?' exclaimed some of our men in indignation, when they sighted red in the enemy ranks. However, the Sicilians who overheard them calmed them down, telling them that the Neapolitan officers also wore red trousers.

The Neapolitan snipers who had crawled down through the rows of prickly-pear bushes were the first to fire.

'Hold your fire. Do not reply to their fire!' shouted out the captains, but the bullets passed over our heads with such a provocative whine that it was impossible to stay still. One shot was heard, then another, and another, until finally the call to arms was sounded out, followed by the order to charge; it came from the General's own trumpeter.

The plain was rapidly crossed, the first enemy line broken....

I saw Garibaldi there on foot, his sheathed sword over his right shoulder, going slowly forward, keeping the whole action in view.

Our men were falling around him, with those wearing the red shirt falling in great numbers. Bixio galloped up to shelter him with his horse, and pulling him behind his mount, shouted at him:

'General, is this how you wish to die?'

'Could I die better than for my country?'

Rifle fire could be heard intermittently; the Royalist forces started rolling down boulders and it was said that even the General had been struck by one.

Near to me Missori, commander of the Scouts, with his left eye all bloody and bruised, seemed to be listening attentively to the noises floating down from the hilltop. We could hear the heavy tramp of the battalions and thousands of voices, like waves on an angry sea, shouting from time to time – 'Long live the King!

Sirtori, dressed in black, with a flash of red shirt showing under his collar, had rips in his clothes from the bullets, but no wounds. Impassive, riding whip in hand, he seemed indifferent to the commotion.

The great, supreme clash came when the Valparaiso banner, passed from hand to hand until it came to Schiaffino, was seen to wave from side to side a few moments in the midst of a dreadful, desperate struggle and then go down. Giovan Maria Damiani of the Scouts was able to seize hold of it by one of the ribbons. He and his rearing horse, in that tangle of friends and enemies, formed a group reminiscent of a Michelangelo.

One of them was loading the muzzle-loader with handfuls of bullets and stones, then he clambered up and fired at will. Short, thin, filthy, we saw him from below tearing his bare shins on the scrub, which gave off a nauseating cemetery odour.

The courage of those monks, every last one of them! I saw one receive a wound in the thigh, pull the pellet from his flesh then continue firing.

During the battle, we could see crowds of peasants intently watching the spectacle from the crags around us. From time to time, they uttered screams which terrified our common enemy.

An icy wind got up...
In an instant all was covered in darkness...

THREE

Morti Sacrata

> Tristes presentimientos de lo que
> ha de acontecer.
> (Dark forebodings of what will
> come to pass.)
>
> Goya, *The Disasters of War*

In Alcara Li Fusi, above the Nebrodi Mountains, 13 May 1860.
   *... ad aridas profectus cautes, siti enectus fontem poposcit, monitusque
baculo ferire silicem, e saxo rivum ...*
   Shit, dried shit, no trace of water, shit on the path between the
rocks, cow shit like bread, mule shit like onions, goat shit like
olives, staff strokes on the ground, and a hollow ring from the
empty, dangling gourd. He was spitting foamy saliva. Saint
Nicolas, Nicolas the Betrothed, miracle worker – there's a good
tale for gullible peasants; virgin, virgin, and what of it? Did you
have it after all, saint? A hermit and saint from fear of the cunt, a
life of roots, peelings, herbs, grubs, grasshoppers, snails, hair-
shirt and the lash, knees on flintstones, sackcloth and ashes,
parchment books, Paracletics, Menologies, a rod with a cross,
skin and bone, on your knees like a straw puppet due for incineration in the cave, *per poenitentiam instar lucernae ardentis ante Deum*,
a fugitive from your father's house on the eve of the wedding and
an anchorite in the Calanna cave for thirty years, having abandoned to a widow's life a fresh, young, intact virgin endowed
with cash and jewels, and why? And yes, a native of Adrano, that
town of fair-skinned males, of displaced, slack-arsed Greeks.
   'Eh, ah,' head turned upwards, this way and that, eyes protruding from sockets at the cawing of the crows and woodpigeons

forced out of their holes in the Crasto, Moele, Cresia, Lemina and Pasci rocks, threatening the valley, gliding upwards in the violet skies. It was the month of May. The evening of the vigil of the feast commemorating the great event in the sixteenth century after seven months without rain: the people invoked the cowled skeleton with book and cross in the glass case perched on an ass's back, led him through fields and along pathways. Look, holy man, blessed hermit, see the fields without grass, animals starving, shrubs burned. It was at that moment that a cloud rose up from the sea, filled the sky and poured gentle, copious rain on the land: dust, dull roar, battering of wind, splash of raindrops on glass case, rancid stench of animals, men, canvases, faces and hands in the air, opened mouths with tongues hanging out. *Sint benedictae mammae quas suxisti et benedictus venter qui te gestavit.*

'Eh, ah?' to the giant gryphons overhead, called vultures by the shepherds.

The sun beyond San Fratello, on the far side of the crest of the mountain, sent out its rays of old Byzantine gold towards the heights, towards the thick broom, mint, fennel, rosemary, oleander and basil, buds of wild rose, gurgle of water in the Stella valley gushing down over rocks and through gorges in the Rosmarino, to torment the Basilian lay friar on the road to Alcara, alms and penitence, dark, bony, bent double, parched with thirst.

In the cave to guard your rotted, powdering bones, I too turned hermit because of the wretched appetites of this great, blind beast, this satan which gnaws at me between the legs. I hid in the cave for years, disguising myself with a beard and a habit to avoid a knife in the guts or a bullet in the back. Was this sin, celibate boy, was this sin? She screamed out, the hell-hag, she screamed out with pain and brought them running into the woods with pitchforks. And what sin can there be, Lucifer, if a great devil has taken up position beneath my belly?

'Ah, oh, ah!' – his satchel entangled in the briars, he tugs and lashes behind him with the staff, without turning round. '*Vade retro*, Satan, you bastard!' – and off he runs, on callus-hard feet, over stone and thistle, doubling over boulders at the roadside to draw breath.

A gryphon, immense over his head, smooth female thighs,

scabs under the wings, ticks, round verminous eye, drops with unmoving, outstretched wings, holding some object in its beak – a gourd, flask or pitcher of fresh water? It opens its beak and the pitcher shatters in pieces on the stone, gurgle of lost water, clench of claws, beak, flap of wings, screeching. The hermit shields his head with the bag, rolls blindly onto the ground with the gryphon, claws on his chest, pressing heavily down, jabbing, beak between his legs. The hermit foams, voice frozen in his throat, sweat and trembling in his bones. Then he screams in the silence of the dusk on the valley, loses consciousness.

Now, as he emerges from sleep, the thumping of irons in his temples, the insistent, rhythmic beat of hammers on anvil, the scraping of metals, the hiss of white-hot steel in water, the groan of bellows, human voices yelling, laughter, the heavy breathlessness of exhaustion. Was this hell? He was still lying under the fig tree, as though dead. He opened first one eye then the other to find himself in a clearing in front of a strange, previously unseen smithy, at Santa Marecuma, with a pen for animals concealed between the oak trees. Outside, Sguro and Malandro, two villains known for strength of arm and for brutality, naked torsos running with sweat, beat swiftly and joyfully on the anvil. And Caco, Scippateste, Carcagnintra, Casta, Mita, Inferno, Misterio and Milinciana, black with the sun and the coal, oiled rusty rifles, cast lead, filled cartridges, filed bullets, stoked irons, pumped bellows, toiled, while over at the whetstone others honed scythes, axes, pitchforks, hoes, knives, shears. Was it April for the hunt, June for the harvest, August for the sheepshearing, October for the woodcutting or December for the slaughter of sheep and pigs?

'Pigs for all seasons, Brother Nunzio.'

'They're plentiful then.'

'Plentiful.'

'Offal, sausages, ribs, salames, fats, lard, ah, what an abundance there will be this year!'

'Even for you, Brother Nunzio.'

'The hermit does not eat.'

'He licks.'

'Blood.'

'Of beech martens.'

'Who suck the blood of rabbits.' They laughed. And the flaming irons were red lights in the gathering evening, and sparks flashed from the honed blades.

'Water, sons,' begged the hermit.

'Water, water for Brother Nunzio.'

The pitcher from hand to hand, serious, charitable looks, and the hermit put it to his mouth, gripping the handles feverishly. His Adam's apple bounced wildly in his gullet. He spewed it out, soaking beard and habit.

'It's vinegar, you swine, vinegar!'

'Vinegar?'

'Vinegar?'

'A miracle!'

'The hermit's a saint.'

'He's changed water to vinegar.'

'Blessed Brother Nunzio!'

'He had a vision by the roadside.'

'And cried out in rapture and delight.'

'And lost consciousness.'

'And the control of his bladder.'

'Swine, satanic tongues, swine!' – under his breath. A humble, submissive smile. 'You not going down to the village, not going to the feast at San Nicola tomorrow?'

'We'll give it a miss this time, Brother Nunzio. Look at the work we've got on.'

'Work?'

'Work.'

'We'll have our feast day next Thursday.'

'Your feast?'

'A big feast.'

'The Ascension.'

'Of Our Lord.'

'And Saviour, Jesus Christ.'

'Amen.'

'Come down from your hermitage, Brother Nunzio, and you'll see for your yourself.'

'Laus Deo,' said the hermit, as he moved towards the road.

The clatter of the irons drowned out the words of the shepherds.

In the Paratica district, in the Church of the Capuchins, desiccated corpses upright in niches in the crypt, necks twisted, mouths gaping, yells, cackles, gloves and slippers, saltpetre, oakum, hollow eye-sockets – it was already night, pierced by occasional lights in the houses and in the streets of the town.

At the Mandrazza crossroads, in the district called Palo – a collection of night-pots and bedpans, of filth and grease, of discharge of kidneys and innards – he, crouching, habit up to the waist, emptied his bowels of what he had picked up on the pathway. Stench of black death in swirling evening breezes sweeping down from Rocazzo, up from Rosmarino, rabble and beasts, pawing dogs, wild pigs rooting in the mire, mice scrabbling on piled excrement. Palo, place of shame and ignominy, once home of blasphemers and heretics, who, fettered, scourged and garrotted, dropped their shit there. Holy the Office that disposed of them. To dispose of those beasts at the smithy hidden among the oak trees, Satan's bastards, to seize their goods, wives, children, animals, to pull down their houses, to demolish the smithy! As had been done to one Matteo, whose house once stood on Via Forno. ON THIS SPOT STOOD THE DWELLING PLACE OF MATTEO CARRUBA DEMOLISHED BY ORDER OF THE HOLY OFFICE IN PUNISHMENT FOR HIS OFFENCE IN INSULTING FRIAR AUGUSTINO OF URBINO, CAPTAIN OF THE SAID HOLY OFFICE. Most holy. And had not the poor hermit, the lay monk, been himself maltreated by those jailbirds?

Under castle Turio, on the Abate square, the seven mouths of the fountain sang, *Arcara hoc placido splendida fonte bibit,* and directly underneath the huge bowl with overturned millstones, broken columns and capitals, the urge to plunge in up to the neck, but only over arms, legs and shameful parts, to gulp water to assuage the burning thirst and fill the gourd as reserve. Clean and fresh on the piazza, people seated in the shade on the stone seat against the wall of the Cathedral of the Assumption, the pendulum tower clock standing at three o'clock at night, the old sundial below a blank stain giving no time, the lamplighter rod in hand, Don Turi Harra, Don Ciccio Papa, the civic courier, Cola Zaiti, steward at the Nobles' Club and Don Tano Manzo, the sacristan. Buzz of talk, sighs and groans, a glance into the tavern from which voices, shouts, glasses shattering, gleaming lights spilled out through the door above the piazza as though from a furnace.

'Laus Deo.'

'Lau.'

'Late tonight, Brother Nunzio.'

'Late leaving the cave. What are those children of God doing?'

'Celebrating.'

'What?'

'Haven't you heard the news?'

'Some one called Garibardo... or Garibaldi...'

'Who is this person?'

'A brigand. An enemy of God and of His Majesty the King, whom God protect. He has landed in Sicily, to unleash revolution, a new '48.'

'He butchers nuns and burns convents, sacks churches, harries the nobles and protects the scum of society.'

'Who go round saying that he has come to give them justice and land.'

Swift sign of the cross, joined hands, head bowed and low murmur of the Lord's Prayer.

'Amen.'

Nimbly, glancing in front, behind, in every nook and cranny, over to the isolated Church of Calvary. A dash into the porch with the speed of a bat circling columns, a furious push at the portal and inner door, an opening and furtive closing, deep sigh inside the nave of the church.

In the centre, a coffin of white planks on a trestle surrounded by four candles in holders at the corners.

'Evil tidings!'

In his recess, which was the altar of the Virgin of the Seven Dolours, the resting place for the night, with cushion, covers, veils, altar-cloths.

He sat on the steps. From his bag came bread, cheese, beans, water from the gourd. Satisfied, yawning, he stretched out and lay back to sleep. The gleam, in the movement of the candle flame, of the copper handles of the coffin, of the pedestal fashioned like gryphon claws, of the seven golden hilts of the swords arrayed on a black velvet mantle piercing the heart of the Virgin Mary, of the staring silver eyes, of the fixed eye, of eyes, of flaming hearts, of ascending and descending brass pipes above the organ. Beyond the lights, in the shadow of the ceiling and the walls, a cascade of sneering skulls, a flight of crossed kneebones, a trembling mass of skeletons rising from under slabs, from arches, from tombs, emerging from graves, angels seen side on, with membraned wings, blowing trumpets...

'Evil tidings!' – and he turned on his back and caressed the devil, which in the softness of the resting place had hardened and stiffened.

Sharp screams of terror, lamentations, convulsive weeping made him waken with a start in the light of the false dawn.

'Blessed Lucifer, what is this screeching?'

The opened coffin, a girl dressed in virginal white cowering on the ground beside it, trembling in panic.

'Quiet, girl...'

'Help me, have mercy...!' crawling on the ground, snatching with trembling hands the hem of the habit, clutching his legs. Raised up by the armpits, she fell back limply onto the flooring.

He took her in his arms and carried her bodily to the recess.

She declined water.

'Call help, hermit, call my father, my brothers...'

Bending over her, his eyes sunken and glistening, a quivering smile uncovering rows of teeth in the midst of the pitch black of his beard.

'Be good, maiden.'

Saints Placido and Lione.

Yes, stay still.

And what is this, by the veil of the Our Lady?

Caressing lightly, with dark, bony hands, her hair and cheeks.

> *Morti sacrata,*
> Consecrated to death
> It is sacrilege to return.
> This is the law, the law
> *Nunquam vivi vocare,*

Call no human creature
Not father, mother, brother
Under pain of hell
Do you understand, dead girl?
At anima partuta
Non licei titubo,
Spolia surrecta
Morta reverterit.
Amen.

And he grabbed her by the knees, prizing them apart with his fingers, forcing them open.

'Mercy, Mother of God...' clambering free from the recess, running madly through the church. 'Help, everybody, help, people, Mother of God come to my aid.'

The hermit pursued her with the processional crucifix, and with one blow of the heavy iron arm cut off the cry in her throat, bringing her lifeless to the ground.

In his recess, he stripped her to the waist and while still warm, possessed her.

He re-arranged the body in the coffin, hands joined and rosary beads intertwined in the fingers, picked up the lid and held it a moment over the coffin. He brought a candle close to the opening and peered in.

'Consecrated to death,' he murmured. He released his grip, and the sound of the lid falling echoed like thunder through the vaults.

Gunfire and fanfares, a concert of bells, cocks crowing and dogs barking, donkeys and asses braying in the May sun, which pierced and stung the eyes after the darkness.

The hermit raced through the back streets, hiding behind wall after wall and made his escape along the alleyways. Panting, breathless, he emerged onto a piazza festooned with banners, flags, drapes, entered the cathedral at the consecration and went straight to the altar. Arms outstretched, eyes turned towards heaven, he fell on his knees facing the congregation.

'Dark forebodings of bitter events rend asunder my heart and mind,' he declaimed in the silence. 'I have in my nostrils the scent of blood, iron, fire... Death. Nobles and working men of Alcara,

arouse yourselves, prepare yourselves! To Santa Marecuma.'
And he stopped. A murmur rose up from the nave. The officiat-
ing priest, Father Adorno, bedecked in white and gold cope,
turned abruptly and stood rooted to the spot, the chalice and host
still raised aloft, the rose window a radiant halo around his head.

The shepherds at the back, beside the holy-water font, smiled
and exchanged glances. The women, already on their knees,
prostrated themselves, invoking with ejaculations and breast-
beating Saint Calogero of Fitalia, Saint Laurence of Frazzano,
Saint Blaise of Caronia, Saint Philip of Fragala, Saint Thecla,
Saint Mary of Tindaro, of Capo d'Orlando, of the Palati and
Maniace.

'Solitude and deprivation have buggered his mind,' murmured
the notary Don Giuseppe Bartolo, Mayor of Alcara, to his son
Ignazio, the teacher, who was at his side. They were in the first
row with the Chiuppa, the Capito, the Manca, the Gentile, the
Artino and Lanza families, the solid phalanx of the notables of the
town, administrators of the wealth of San Nicola and San Pantaleo, a finger in every pie, usurpers of the freehold lands, each
one as overbearing and arrogant as though he were the heir of the
Palizzi or the Cardona.

'Always was a bit queer, papa. Suffers from epilepsy.'

'Where's he from?'

'Some say from Bronte, some from Galati or Tortorici. Some
say he's an educated man, others that he's from the gutter. But
everybody knows that he went into hiding in his hermitage
because of some business concerning a woman.'

'A woman! That bag of skin and bones.'

'They say he has a tool like an ass's.'

'An ass's head, more like. And the shoulders of a bird of ill
omen.'

The hermit ran from the altar, fled along the aisle, rushed into
the sun-soaked piazza, where a sudden attack of his ailment
brought him to the ground with a scream.

FOUR

Val Demone

In Sant'Agata di Militello, 15 May 1860.

From Canna Melata, from the squares around the castle and the church, down through Costa di Pozzo, and even from as far afield as the telegraph office, from Cucco Bello and Vallon di Posta, the whole population made its way down to the harbour. The fishermen were first, well ahead of the muleteers or the carters, to catch sight of the arrival of the mail-boat. Huge and white, with smoke streaming from the funnel and enormous paddle wheels creating a tremendous din as they went round in the water. It passed the mouth of the Furiano and of the Inganno, went round Punta Lena and cast anchor. Directly opposite the tower of the Granza Maniforti castle, within gun range.

'Raimondo, I'm losing my temper,' said Prince Galvano, beating his whip against his boot, to his son who was playing with the tripod telescope on the tower terrace.

'I can see, I can see...'

'What in God's name do you see?'

'A lion...a lion drinking in a stream.'

'What a discovery! That's the coat of arms of the Florio fleet. The name, I want to know the name of the steamer.'

'Siiii...ciiii...leye.'

'Sicileye! Sicileye!! For God's sake! Just what are those priests in the Capizzi college in Bronte teaching you? That's what I want to know.'

Raimondo, heedless of what his father was saying, turned the glass on to the deck and cried out with delight at the sight of the captain, the bosun, the stokers, the sailors, of the passengers scurrying about, locking their cases, looking over the side.

'Sicileye!' repeated Prince Galvano. 'God Almighty! You're going to drive me mad. This is the vessel, the very vessel Mandralisca is to be on. Move yourself, go and tell Matafu to get down and meet him at the quayside.'

Raimondo did not move. He stayed where he was, bent over, glued to the telescope. Prince Galvano gave him a sharp smack on the buttocks with his whip. Raimondo straightened up smartly, looked at his father in bewilderment, and then moved, rubbing his bottom, down the spiral staircase towards the courtyard. The Prince, having looked around him to make sure that he was alone and that there were no indiscreet eyes to report his weakness, positioned himself in front of the tripod; he spread out his legs, leaned forward, placed one hand over his left eye and put the right eye against the eyeglass. His mouth dropped open with amazement. He raised the hand holding the whip, and began lashing out in the air as though to strike at the figures who were appearing before him in their natural size. The leather thong collided with the front lens of the telescope, bringing it to the ground with a metallic clatter, while the other end was propelled brusquely into the air, sending the Prince's bowler hat flying.

'Goddammit,' he cursed loudly. He bent down to pick up his hat and moved over to the balcony railing, where the ivy from below, having successfully covered the entire curve of the tower, was beginning to make an appearance on its upwards path, growing thicker as it climbed, coating the whole wall and threatening to cover the castle (the lizards and spiders that hid there!)

He looked over to the right, towards the coastline which snaked to the edge of the plains of Torrenova, Rocca and the Cape, furrowed by the Zappulla and Rosmarino rivers, and further on, beyond Capo d'Orlando, Lipari and Vulcano, to the tongues of undivided land stretching on to the Cape of Malazzo; and turned his gaze to the twin islands of Salina and to the cliffs, as clear blue and transparent as sails on the horizon, of Alicuri and Filicuri. On the other side, beyond the headland of Lena, beyond Acquedolci, Torremuzza and Finale, there rose up the three-pointed Rock, shaped like the crown on the fair head of a Norman Roger or William, of that town as old as time which was Cefalu.

'Sheer madness!' said Maniforti to himself. 'Does our eccentric Baron Mandralisca never get sick of travelling?'

He looked again at the steamer; skiffs and launches from the shore had drawn alongside to disembark passengers and luggage, while the townsfolk lining the harbour wall shouted out their greetings.

'Fools and idlers! Look at them trooping out of their offices and workshops to gape at some boat propelled by fire!' murmured Prince Galvano to himself. He turned away from the sea and went down the stairs to the rooms on the floor below.

He heard the horses' hooves and the irons of the carriage wheels on the cobblestones in the courtyard. Galvano looked out of the window and through a gap in the thick roof formed by the leaves of the plane and fig trees, through the thickets in the palm and banana foliage, he glimpsed Mandralisca descending from the coach assisted by the coachman Matafu. Behind them, red in the face and out of breath, weighed down with packages, cases and trunks, a fat manservant.

'Enrico, Enrico,' called the Prince.

'Galvano, Galvano!' came the answering cry from Mandralisca, as he looked up, disoriented, like Adam at the voice of God the Father, to identify his friend above the foliage.

The two friends embraced on the stairs. In the drawing-room they sat facing each other, laughing happily.

'How delightful, how delightful! Maniforti repeated continuously. And, as happened every time the two met – and that occurred once every decade – they relived their days in the boarding school in the Royal Caroline Monastery in Palermo, days now as remote and as crystal clear as a portrait from which the artist has removed every extraneous element the better to bring out the essential traits: the most remarkable faces, the most stentorian voices among the teaching staff; the most brazen and plucky of their schoolmates; the most attractive of the mothers and sisters on visits in the parlour on feast days. The talk would then turn to the fate and prospects of their various companions, to fortunes dissipated, to estates gambled away over the turn of a card, to deaths and wills, suicides and murders, the sale of titles, the extinction of houses, brilliant careers, engagements and weddings, disease, offspring, grandchildren...

'Life,' concluded Maniforti, as he invariably did on these occasions.

'Ah yes, life,' echoed Mandralisca, who knew only too well that it was not possible with Maniforti to get beyond conversation on individuals, on family rows, on property and interests. Any attempt to widen the conversation to governments, the fate of empires, kingdoms, principalities, to war and peace, to rights and the freedom of peoples would have been futile. Above the fireplace he saw the coat of arms of the illustrious family from which Galvano traced his descent: a lion rampant, two feet on the ground and two pawing the air.

'Just how,' wondered Mandralisca, 'just how did those ancestors of ours become nobles, through having attended to their own interests or to those of others? If the first hypothesis is true – and it is – the whole of humanity deserves the status of nobility ... or else, alas! we are all equally ignoble!... With a few exceptions,' admitted Mandralisca. And his mind ran to the poets, the scientists, the philosophers, the men of learning, detached and indifferent to the struggle to accumulate wealth...

'No, no, never!' he said to himself. 'There is invariably someone behind them, a father or a patron, who has drudged and laboured to put food in their bellies, to give them the leisure to versify, to pursue research, ideas, experiments. And what about me?' he thought. 'If I hadn't received from my father Colombo, Giarrizzello, Musa and all the other estates, would I have been able to indulge myself with pursuing birds, rooting around for palmiped eggs and snails, or with collecting fragments, art treasures, coins, paintings?' His thought moved to his pride and joy, Antonello's portrait of the Unknown Man. And, from the face of the unknown man, it passed naturally to the living, incisive, idiosyncratic face of an unknown mariner, of a wily merchant, of a fiery revolutionary...

'Perhaps, perhaps Interdonato is a noble man...' concluded Mandralisca. And he looked over the balcony, into the emptiness, without seeing the crown of hills which rose up between the sky and the plateau on which this castle and the surrounding houses stood. On the right was San Fratello, in the form of a headless sphinx, Inganno valley, the Sanguinera, Vallebruca,

Serra Aragona and the peak of San Basilio sopra Tiranni (it was over there, in an opulent villa, that a celebrated Minister of Police from the court of the Sovereign King Ferdinand took refuge, to enjoy his declining years and to compose his memoirs; Vicarioto by name – and Vicarioto by nature, added the local people, in whose language *vicaria* meant prison, residence of the criminal evildoer; and in comparison with Vicarioto – servant of the servants of a corrupt State, boss of bosses of police gangsters – the people languishing in the dungeons, cells or coops of any *vicaria* in Noto, Procida, Nisida, Trapani, Milazzo, Favignana or elsewhere were to be numbered amongst the holiest and most saintly of men, worthy of comparison with Christ scourged at the pillar). On the left was Mount Scurzi, bare of vegetation, and San Marco thick with houses clinging precariously to its sides; behind could be made out the granite formations overhanging the ancient town called Alcara.

'What's the matter, Enrico? Not feeling well?'

'Oh, no,' replied Mandralisca, rousing himself. 'Just a bit of dizziness, nothing else. The journey, you know.'

'Bon, bon,' said Maniforti. 'We'll go to dinner in a short while and once you've had a good night's sleep you'll be yourself again.'

'Just what I need. Tomorrow I'll make an early start for Alcara.'

'So soon?'

'Afraid so. Baron Manca's expecting me.'

'Do you mind, Enrico, if I ask you a question? What are you up to in that wild village of goatherds? If it's good hunting you're after, I would advise the woods round Caronia, or those other ones even closer at hand at Miraglia. That's where we go, Scalea and I, and sometimes the Pignatelli, Piccolo, Salerno, Cupani come along too.'

'Hunting... I suppose it is a kind of hunting, but not for quails, pheasants or rabbits. I'm on the hunt for snails.'

'Snails?' asked Prince Galvano and there was a touch of terror in his voice. 'If that's all it is I'll have them bring all the basketfuls you can carry.'

'No, no, I'm very grateful...' said Mandralisca smiling.

'These are special snails. I have to search them out by myself, my dear Galvano. They are not for eating. On the contrary, I am so familiar with them, these little creatures, that the idea of eating them is quite upsetting.' And he gave a full explanation to Prince Galvano, who for a time believed him deranged. 'These are the snails I need to catalogue for the study of the general malacology of Sicily I have been engaged on for years. Baron Andrea Bivona and I are working together, and we are just putting the final touches to it.'

'Ah, I see,' said Prince Galvano. 'But there's no shortage of snails round here. I don't see the need to go as far as Alcara.'

'No, no... I'm interested in those that flourish in the mountain streams, and in the springs and caves, like the Lauro cave under Mount Crasto.'

'Bon, bon,' capitulated Galvano. 'If it keeps you happy. Tomorrow the carriage will be waiting at first light. It's a hard road, uphill all the way, full of twists and turns as far as Militello Rosmarino. Then from there to Alcara it gets a bit more straight and flat.'

'Papa, papa!' screamed Raimondo, making his entrance, but he checked himself and made a deep bow to the guest he saw with his father.

'Come, introduce yourself to Baron Mandralisca, a very dear childhood friend of mine,' said Galvano. Raimondo went over to the armchair where Mandralisca was seated, bent forwards offering for a kiss a forehead full of the blackheads and pimples of adolescence.

'How old are you?' asked Mandralisca.

'Thirteen and a half,' replied Raimondo proudly, drawing himself up to his full height, making himself seem longer and thinner than he was, like a cucumber or courgette with its roots in a jar of water.

'What subjects do you take?'

'Rhetoric, ethics, etiquette, heraldry, solfa, fencing, calculus, humanity and *français*.'

'Good lad, well done!' Mandralisca complimented him with a chuckle.

'He's attending the Capizzi College,' added his father. 'I brought him home just now because he's suffering from a form of anaemia. He needs fresh air, sun, sea and... he'll need to put on a bit of weight, get some flesh on those bones.'

'Indeed, indeed,' agreed Mandralisca. 'And his mother, your good wife?'

'In Palermo, Palermo! She won't move from there. She says that once she's away from Palermo, she gets depressed. Here she feels in exile, in the middle of a desert... You know how pig-headed the whole Sutera family always was... But let's say no more about it.' He turned to his son who was standing there rooted to the spot, not missing a word. 'What is it, Raimondo? What brought you in here?'

'Papa, papa,' began Raimondo, growing as excited as before. 'They've brought another prisoner into the cellars.'

'All right, all right,' said Prince Galvano. 'How many times have I told you to keep away from the courtyard?'

'But papa, I was with Matafu and the Baron's Cefalu servant. He spat at me! He passed right in front of us between two guards, he stared at me and then he spat at me. Look, look, you can still see where it's wet.' Raimondo showed Galvano the black, round damp patch on his green velvet jacket.

'Go and get changed. It's nearly time for dinner anyway,' said Galvano in annoyance.

'But the guards threw him to the ground, they kicked him and dragged him away. Rosario, the man from Cefalu, kept on saying "Mamma mia, mamma mia!" and ran away.' And he laughed, looking over at Mandralisca.

'I won't tell you again. Go and get changed,' Prince Galvano raised his voice impatiently.

'A bunch of highwaymen, footpads, pickpockets, brigands,' began Maniforti as soon as the boy was out of earshot. 'They steal anything they can lay their hands on – firewood, acorns, herbs, olives, goats, pigs – if they got the chance they'd be in the house thieving the food from the plates we eat off. Do you understand now why I left Palermo and why I am so determined to stay here, on my lands? There's not a single field-guard, gamekeeper or servant, no matter how reliable, who's good enough to compensate for the master's absence. These are desperate, anarchic times . . . there are no laws, no sentences, no punishments capable of deterring this growing band of robbers! And they hate you, God damn them, they even have the gall to spit at you!' As he spoke, Prince Galvano grew increasingly apoplectic. 'They'll learn, mark my words, all these fine ladies and gentlemen disporting themselves in Palermo just now!' His rage was unbounded. 'They'll learn, when they find themselves stripped of everything except eyes for shedding tears.'

Whack! Whack! Whack! There: a flash of white light followed by the dark red of dungeon darkness, taste of salt, of aloes and potassium, smell of jackets piled up, shock and bewilderment, a sudden blow and fury rising from the nerves and veins burning with fear and pain.

'No! Why? Why?' Cries, crouched in a corner of the 'Villa of the Papyri', arms flailing against the *brutes* who beat him repeatedly on the forehead, on the stomach, on the nose, on the face, with iron bars, with their knees and hands. His screams brought some quarrymen out from tunnels nearby, and the labourers stood and stared.

'Bastard, shitface, arsehole,' shouted the two policemen as they carried on beating him. The hound on the chain bared its teeth, growled, strained at its spiked collar, scratched at the ground with its paws.

They secured his wrists with handcuffs. Under the blue sky, between Resina and the sea, between the white of the marble, the red of the bricks and the green of the pines, he felt his legs buckle, his mind cloud over and drift into unconsciousness.

'We know who you are! You gave refuge in your house last November to dangerous scoundrels and fomenters of unrest and sedition against His Sacred Majesty and the Sovereign Order. In '48, you were a deputy with that Ruggiero Settimo who is in hiding in Malta, the so-called President of a comic opera kingdom, and you've never retracted your belief in subversion. So, Mandralisca, these are the main charges,' stated Inspector Condo in San Ferdinando palace, flicking through his papers. 'Confess: what were you planning to do in the capital?'

'To visit the excavations in Herculaneum...'

'You'd be better employed thinking of the grave you're digging for yourself this very minute. You haven't forgotten Spinuzza and Bentivegna, have you? You don't, by any chance, know anything about the explosions on the *Carlo III*, or at the ammunition dump?'

'I came to visit...'

'Shut up! We understand. You can thank your destiny and the benevolence of the Minister for Sicilian Affairs, Cavaliere Cassini. What little favour can you have done him? You or your lady wife?'

He jumped to his feet, and tied up as he was, made to throw himself on the Inspector, but the *brutes*, standing behind him, laid hands on him contemptuously and forced him back down onto the chair.

'You will be immediately taken back in chains to your home town, with the order not to set foot outside it for two years!' said Condo, writing as he spoke. He closed the file, slapped his hand down on top of it and told the two guards to take him out.

Maniforti talked and talked while Mandralisca, deaf to the words that were being spoken, began to scrutinise his face, red with dull rage, the bulging veins of the neck, the quiver of the upper lip, the watery eye, the excited tapping of the whip against the boot (an elegant but robust riding whip, with handle and eyelet of morocco leather, steel tip shining like the point of a sword).

Concentrating on the head, Mandralisca observed him with the alert attention which, through his Neer and Blunt compound microscope, he normally devoted to the acephala and gasteropoda of the most strange and bizarre genuses, families or species. He managed to rip aside, dissolve, evaporate the thick veil, the layers of age-old incrustation clustered like mosses on a stone, layers formed from long acquaintance, routine, familiarity and perhaps even fondness; he had the impression of focusing on him, of really seeing him for the first time. Objectively. And he had a sudden sense of alienation, of distance and finally of repulsion which clouded, like an unexpected movement at the bottom of a pond, the objective, cold, serene eye of a few moments before.

The church clock struck a quarter past four, making Mandralisca leap from his bed, instantly wide awake and clear-headed. From the flickering candle on the bedside cabinet, quivering smoky shafts of uncertain light played around the cover of the book *On Remedies for the Disease of the Air in Many Regions of Sicily* by Giulio Carapezza, and around the pocket watch and the pince-nez lying beside it. He opened the door of the balcony overlooking the sea, stepped on to the terrace, where the sweetish scent of datura met him on the threshold. He walked over to the railing to breathe the purer, clearer air of the morning. He heard the dull hoot, like that of a man snoring in sleep, of an old owl hidden in some corner of the tower. The noises of the boats, the splash of the oars, the tossing of the ropes, the drag of the hull, all the varied sounds of the fishing fleet as it made its early morning return to port, floated up from the shore. A crescent daytime moon, bereft of all enchantment, hung over the horizon, and in the pale, opalescent light Mandralisca saw the sirens, the huge eyes, the madonnas, the red and yellow bands, the triangles and lozenges on the prow and sides of the boats. The silent fishermen went about the business of passing the fish baskets from hand to hand, hanging out the nets, winding up the tackle and laying out the fishing lamps on the shingle.

'What an unhappy, funereal ritual!' observed Mandralisca.

He went back inside. He crossed the room and opened the window on the courtyard side, where the thick vegetation still immersed in silence kept daylight at bay. A pink rose opened out to the east, above the tiles of the church. A few moments later he heard the scraping of horses' hooves on the cobblestones. When he went downstairs, he found Rosario and Matafu deep in conversation, ready and waiting for him beside the carriage. Morning had broken.

'A fine day, your Excellency,' they trilled in unison.

'Time to go,' said Mandralisca, in the highest of spirits.

'Eau devant, vaint darrier e la mart arba chi v'arcuogghi tucc!' came a voice from the bottom of the courtyard.

'Who was that?' asked Mandralisca.

'The prisoner,' replied Rosario and Matafu.

'What did he say? What did it mean?'

'Water before you, wind behind and may blind death take one and all!' explained Matafu.

Mandralisca turned to look. A shadow could be made out against the round wall, between the stables and the storehouses, where the oil jars, the sacks of wheat and shelves of cheese were kept. His curiosity aroused, Mandralisca went over to the man.

'No, your Excellency, no!' implored Rosario. 'He's a devil from hell.'

The man, barefoot, naked to the waist, was bound hand and foot; his wrists were chained above his head to an iron ring in the wall, used for securing horses and mules.

When Mandralisca stood in front of him, the man laughed insolently and contemptuously in his face. He was a mere boy, no more than twenty years old, sturdy and tall, blue eyes, face the colour of baked brick, hair curly, unkempt and as golden as the metal earring in his right ear.

'What did you do?' asked Mandralisca.

'Ammazzeu n'agnieu pi li muntegni, rabba sanza patran...'

'What are you saying,' asked Mandralisca, who did not understand that strange language.

The man made no reply, and laughed at him once more. 'I killed a lamb on the mountain, a thing with no master,' explained Matafu.

Mandralisca then noticed that the man's skin was flayed, his blood hard and clotted, his shoulders, chest and sides disfigured by black and purple marks; an *ecce homo*, a Saint Sebastian totally enveloped at that instant (like a statue of Parian marble, an alabaster by Gaggini or Laurana) in the golden shower of sunrays which entered through an opening in the roof of leaves and touched his breast.

'Who was it?' Mandralisca asked him compassionately.

'U principeu di mad, curnui vecch! Chi si pigghiessu i dijievu di Vurchien tucc i ricch, e a carpa di maza i mazzirran.'

Mandralisca picked out only a word sounding like 'prince', and instinctively took a step back.

'A prince of shit, you old bastard! The devils of Vulcano take all rich men, and beat them to death with their clubs.' The voice was again Matafu's.

'Damn!' exclaimed Mandralisca under his breath. 'The coward!' The delicate hand, gloved in white cotton, clasping the red handle of the twined, ox gut whip, the pale face so easily moved to apoplexy, appeared before his eyes; he felt a motion of nausea for something in that Granza Maniforti which he could not clearly decipher. He looked back at the prisoner. The savage smiled at him with the same contempt. Mandralisca, moved by the awkwardness he himself felt, took three pieces of silver out of his pocket and approached the man to hand them over. As though bitten by a viper, the prisoner lashed out: 'Va', va', pri sant'Arfin! Firrijia, vaa, curnui cam tucc! Jiea suogn zappuner, sanfrarideu, ni bagascia au dimuosinant!'

'Go away, go away, by Saint Alfio! Get out, go away, you're a bastard like all the rest! I work the fields, I'm from San Fratello, I'm no whore or beggar.' Matafu spoke hesitantly. Mandralisca turned on his heels and moved smartly towards the carriage.

'Move, move!' he ordered, jumping aboard. 'Let's go, at once!'

'Yaaaaa,' bawled Matafu, cracking his whip in the air.

Before the coach exited through the castle gate, Mandralisca turned back for a last look, through the lunette, at that man tied to the wall.

When they reached Vallon di Posta, Mandralisca leaned forward towards the coachman's seat to ask Matafu: 'Where's he say he was from?'

'Who, your Excellency?'

'The prisoner.'

'Ah, San Fratello, God save us. Wild people, curious folk, not like anyone else. They speak a strange, foreign language.'

Mandralisca remembered that San Fratello was one of the Lombard villages of Val Demone, like Piazza, Aidone, Sperlinga, Nicosia... Apollonia for the Byzantine Stephen, *plesion Alontinon cai tes Cales Actes*, San Marco or Caronia, and that Val Demone had become *Dimnasc, Demenna, Demona, cora demennon*. (Beleaguered in the castle, the townspeople took milk from nursing mothers, made cheese, and lowered it down to the besieging forces to show how abundant were their provisions. Alfio, Cirino, Filadelfio, children of nomads, of barbarians, of hordes from Emilia and Lombardy, in the pay of Ruggero and Adelasia – at Fragalà, in fulfilment of his vow, the mercenary commander left his standard – Jews in the Good Friday procession, masters of woodland lore, purple spinning tops, angels of sulphur and wine, dancers to golden trumpets and clanking chains. And who in the island of the romance language transmitted by Gallic and Teutonic tongues, who could ever understand that archaic, vulgar language of yours, who could fathom that not wholly destroyed vernacular?)

Mandralisca lounged back against the shoulder-rest, pulled up the shawl he had over his legs so as to cover his chest, huddled into the corner and lost himself in a reverie of solitude and bewilderment.

They passed Terreforti and Orecchiazzi, Astasi and Monte Scurzi. On the dizzy curves overhanging the valley which sloped sharply down to the narrow, rock-lined riverbed of the Rosmarino (the women stone-carriers, with their baskets on their heads, could be spotted as they picked their way along the riverside path), Rosario cried out in terror, while Matafu thoroughly enjoyed himself cracking the whip and making the two horses go faster and faster.

'That's San Marco D'Aliunto,' said Matafu to Rosario, pointing out a village with a hundred or so monasteries and churches, clinging to the hilltop on the far side of the valley. 'And down there that's Torrenova, and then there's the plain and you can just make out Capo D'Orlando in the distance.'

'How lovely, beautiful, all very pretty,' trilled Rosario, confronted with the sight of those hills, valleys, plains, and of the sea and coastline spread ahead of them. Matafu went on: 'There is a jingle repeated round here:

> Capu D'Orlannu a Munti Piddirinnu
> Biati l'occhi che vi vidirannu.'

'Blessed are the eyes which daily see, Capo D'Orlando and Monte Pellegrino,' he explained, puffing himself out, and injuring the pride of the Baron's servant, who retorted to the coachman,

who had never travelled, never seen anything apart from a few
woods, some odd bits of countryside and old, dilapidated villages, that the huge rock overlooking the great city of Cefalu had
no reason, none at all, to fear comparison with any Monte Pellegrino or with that pimple of a hill called Orlando, which bore the
name of the chivalrous paladin from puppet theatre.

'So no more of your nonsense!' concluded Rosario the Cefalu-
tan, crossing his arms on his chest and sticking his chin out
aggressively, with wounded vanity.

Mandralisca lost patience with the chatter that ricocheted
down from the driving seat to the interior of the coach, with the
back and forth of the cavernous, catarrh-thick voice of the coachman and the shriller, more strident voice of Rosario Guercio, his
serving man.

They finally reached Militello and rode up to the post-house
behind the Church of the Annunciation to change horses.

'Do you want to get down, your Excellency, have a bite to eat,
stretch your legs a bit?' Rosario asked Mandralisca, sticking his
great head inside the window of the coach.

'Off you go, Rosario, and take the coachman with you,' replied
Mandralisca testily, slipping a coin into Rosario's palm and waving his hand in front of his nose to signify that he did not wish to
be further disturbed.

He had fallen into a mood of dark depression. And so he
remained for the duration of the journey, which took them past
Santa Maria, Montarolo, the Trappeto of Rantu, until they
reached the Rosario, the first church the traveller meets inside
Alcara.

He made an effort to raise his spirits and pretend to feel some
delight and joy at arriving and finally meeting up with his host,
Baron Manca, whom he had never seen in his life and had known
only through correspondence. Mandralisca's ancient mania, his
relentless dedication to research, his inveterate passion for snails,
his pride, his ambition to be recognised one day, soon, throughout the kingdom and beyond, as a scientist, made him open his
lips in a smile when, as Rosario opened the coach door, he stepped lightly onto the flagstones of Piazza San Nicolo Politi in the
centre of the town.

The piazza was bathed in sunshine and had been made ready for some festival. Bunting, banners, lanterns, flags, tapestries, garlands, bouquets, ribbons and drapes had been put up by the townspeople, who gathered round to stare at the coach and at the three strangers, newly arrived from God knows where.

The Cathedral bell tolled midday on the eve of the feast. Mandralisca, blinking in the bright light after the semi-darkness of the coach interior, looked around the piazza and saw emerging from a side street, at the head of a suite of servants and retainers, a little man as round as a barrel, waddling forwards on two bow legs, arms outstretched, a smile etched on a face which glistened as though it had been greased.

'What a disagreeable lot, what an ugly race we are,' he thought to himself as he went forward, smiling, to greet Baron Manca.

FIVE

The Vespers

In Alcara Li Fusi, 16 May 1860.

Peppe Sirna was at Sollazzo Verde, a finger of land cut out of
the estate of the Baron Manca. From dawn he had been toiling
with his pickshovel, stroke after stroke, wheezing, ah ah, over
the tough rocky crust on the side of a sloping hill, with no more
than a midday lump of bread and cheese and a drop of water to
keep him going. Bent double. His shirt and waistcoat soaked
with sweat, a handkerchief round his neck, and that May sun continually biting his back. He worked with fury and passion,
buoyed up by the hope that perhaps soon, tomorrow, who
knows when? this tiny patch of land might... and he had no
other thought in mind. Nothing other than that ancient, familiar
dream, which made him sink into a trance, into forgetfulness of
himself and of his weariness. And Giuseppe Sirna Papa, born in
Alcara, son of Giuseppe, husband of Serafina, twenty-six years
old, no longer knew he was a man... nor did he know anything
of the place, the hour, the season. Only the thud of the hoe on the
earth and on the rocks, and himself standing there, in a state of
dull bewitchment, ah ah, like a blind donkey staggering after the
creak of the buckets in a noria.

But suddenly his hands released their grip on the hoe, his knees
bent, and with a weak groan he fell headlong to the ground. He
heaved a sigh, had the time to utter 'mamma' before he vomited.
He cleaned his ferret-like features and rolled over on his back, his
arms outstretched. He blinked at the sight of the reddening sky
and of the sun falling towards the west. He closed his eyes and
pressed his hand on a heart galloping like a stallion. He raised

himself to a sitting position, wound his arms round his knees and let his head fall forward.

And thus it was that *sitting in perfect immobility, his ears filled with a sound not clearly articulated but redolent of some unstated joy. He sat upright, listening attentively, and recognised festive bells ringing in the distance; a few moments later, he heard the echo from the mountain, repeating the harmony languidly and irregularly and merging with it. Immediately after, he heard the tolling of other bells nearer at hand, they too proclaiming the feast, and then others and others again.* The humble salutation from the town's bells, from the Cathedral, from San Michele, from the Church of the Annunciation, soared through the evening breezes towards the crags and peaks of the mountains, tumbled from slope to slope, swelled through the valleys and, vibrating in the clear, bright crimson air, spread out to fill the plain, the orchards, the fields, the crops, the woodland, the fallow enclosures. The bells of the country churches, the Hermitage and the Rogato sent back their joyous answer. A festive sound. For the feast of the Ascension the following day, the seventeenth May. The poverty-ridden peasants pull off their caps, uncover their heads; nobles and field-guards bow their foreheads. The slow melody of flutes, the low murmur of the Jew's harp, the merry ringing of sheep bells pass unseen between heaven and earth. The pain of toil, the mental strife, the ache in the turbulent breast causing tears to flow, all melt like lumps of honey in the sun, like a knot in silk. All is still, suspended, waiting; the boats, spots of yellow and orange on a sea of circles and rays; the boat with the white sheep, their heads swaying gently over the surface of the waters; the pensive rower; the fond mother embracing the wide-eyed baby. Or else: men, heads bowed, in cardboard trousers and women in long, wood-like, pleated skirts, animals, hayforks stuck in the ground, barrows, spades, hoes, bags overflowing with potatoes and cabbages.

The hoe abandoned on the ground in Sollazzo Verde had a handle covered in vomit. Peppe picked it up, dragged it along the ground then rubbed it on dry clumps of grass. 'To Santa Marecuma...' the thought flashed unbidden into his mind. 'To Santa Marecuma, by God!' he said, abruptly shaking himself. And with instant, decisive, full-hearted conviction, as though abandoning himself to something he had always believed right but over which he had until recently entertained some disabling doubt, he poured on his hands and splashed on his face the last remaining drops of water from the flask. He gathered together his few belongings, picked up his scythe and hoe and set off towards the town with a spring in his step.

The dark blue bulk of the mountains stood out sharply against the pure, Good Friday violet sky. There, deep in the mountains, the blood-red outcrops of the rocks and the narrow-bedded, fast-flowing torrents tumbling down into the rivers could be seen, while at the foot and on the sides, the swaying grey-silver foliage of the olive trees and, here and there on the plateau, the intense fire of the poppies, the yellow of the wheat and the quivering blue of the flax each came into view. The eye could identify the snaking paths, the donkey tracks and footways, as well as the shepherds, the farm hands and the peasants in groups, with asses and goats, making their way home along them, from distant farms, from communal lands, from Mangalavite, Scavioli, Bacco, Lemina, Mura. They proceeded on their way in festive mood, converging on the level plain which led to the hidden valley of Santa Marecuma.

Peppe found himself in the clearing in front of the smithy, where the massed comrades, in twos, threes or larger groups, some leaning against the trunks of trees, others lying on the grass, spoke in rasping voices, with small, quick gestures and much backslapping; all the while spitting, fooling about, making threats, issuing jibes and blasphemous oaths; against absent, distant parties.

'Peppe, Peppe Sirna,' he heard his name called aloud. The speaker was Nino Carcagnintra, who was standing in a group with Cola Vinci, Michele Patroniti, Santo Misterio, Turi Tanticchia and Peppe Tramontana; mates at work and cronies in drink.

'Oh,' replied Peppe, making his way over to join the group.

'And what is this grey colour, this dead face that we see before us, Peppe?' asked Quagliata.

'Nothing.'

'The shits, panic or a slack arse?'

'Ooooh, oooh,' stuttered Peppe in reply. 'Who are you supposed to be, the fearless bandit Testalonga? I've buggered myself once too often; I threw up, up there, on Sollazzo Verde.'

'Come on, Sirna, no more whining!' said Misterio.

'You'll get your colour back tomorrow,' added Tramontana.

'As red as must,' put in Quagliata.

'Red!' they all chorused, and burst into a loud laugh.

And behind their backs others laughed. Peppe wheeled round, laughing in his turn, and there were many of them, perhaps as many as forty or fifty in total, all comrades, friends, acquaintances, some unmoving, silent, arms crossed, others cheerful, exhilarated, leaping about on feet wrapped around with patches of rough cloth. At that moment, three horsemen mounted on three pack animals emerged from the oak woods. Don Ignazio Cozzo was in the middle, with Don Nicolo Vincenzo Lanza and Turi Malandro Frangapane on either side; the first two belonged to the gentry, the last was leader of the farm workers.

The sound of the voices died away one by one, leaving complete silence over the whole gathering.

Don Ignazio spoke.

'Men of Alcara, companions, friends, the time for delay and hesitation is past: the hour of our deliverance is at hand. General Garibaldi has arrived at Alcamo, a village at the very gates of Palermo. The hated Bourbon has finally been chased from this sacred land. It is our duty to see justice done with our own hands on enemies here. Already similar actions are being prepared in every village and town of Sicily. The spirit, the fire, the unshakeable determination to overthrow the tyrant are everywhere in evidence. God, Saint Nicholas, Garibaldi and Victor Emmanuel are with us. To arms! Let neither pity nor cowardice hold back our sword! Men of Alcara, our forebearance has been mighty down the years, our rage is mighty and tomorrow let our courage too be mighty!'

Don Nicolo Vincenzo Lanza, fair-skinned and as thin as a rake, marked his agreement with every word by keeping his head constantly nodding, up and down, in time with the movements of his mount.

Turi Malandro, immobile, head held high, beret half concealing his forehead, one hand in his gunbelt and the other clutching the mule's reins, stared at each in turn, full in the eye.

'Tomorrow,' continued Don Ignazio, 'using the feast as pretext, a detachment of you will march through the village, banging the drum and waving the tricolour. You will invite the citizens to leave their houses, to congregate in the piazza to celebrate, so they will be told (it's only a matter of hours) the seizure of Palermo by General Garibaldi. Each one of you will be there in the piazza, in front of the nobles' club, and when Malandro cries out (this will be the agreed signal) *Viva l'Italia*, you will throw yourselves on the first noble you find. Then... do what you will ...I have nothing to add. Just one last thing. Tonight, at the stroke of midnight, everyone will gather at the Church of the Holy Rosary. The three of us will be there, together with the parish priest, Father Saccone. Each of us will, in the presence of this man of God, swear a solemn oath on the Bible. Until tonight, then. Turi Malandro will now address you.'

Turi remained impassive. Immobile as he was, he moved only his lips, and spoke in grave, measured tones.

'I say this: the signal will be *Justice!* and not *Viva l'Italia*, do you understand? Turi Malandro will cry out *Justice!* I warn you: the easiest thing is the first gesture, the first dagger in the guts when your blood is up. Even a woman could do as much. It is afterwards that the real dance begins. Because afterwards, blood, screams, tears, mercy, promises and entreaties could weaken the toughest liver. I warn you: if one of you, only one, allows himself to give in to suffering or fear, he risks fucking the entire revolution. Now then: if any one of you thinks in all good faith that he could be that one man, let him declare it now, while there is still time. Come now, men, there is no shame in it.'

No one spoke.

'Good,' said Malandro. He went on: 'And to conclude, a disagreement. I am in disagreement with Don Ignazio over that oath. For three reasons: the church has nothing to do with us; the priest is an outsider, of a different race; and we cannot read the gospel. I propose: let us make our oath here, at once.'

And he fell silent.

Don Ignazio replied:

'As regards that *Justice!* I have no objection. Italy and justice are one and the same thing: words. Their only value is what they conceal – the signal. And so *Justice!* it will be. As to courage in the first and subsequent moments, Malandro has my full backing. And may I say how glad I am to see one and all united in their determination not to pull back. Let us now come to the third point... Don Nicolo!' he said, turning furiously towards Lanza at his side. 'What the fuck are you doing? Stop rocking your head like that, you're making me sick!'

A loud laugh went up from the whole assembly. Don Nicolo Vincenzo turned scarlet, bent his shoulders and seemed to crouch down on horseback.

'As I was saying, let's turn to the third point,' continued Don Ignazio. 'The oath. My friends... Nobody is trying to force you to take the sacraments, holy water, the host or the last rites,' and he raised his hand in the air with the index and little finger out-stretched, to ward off the bad luck provoked by the reference to death. 'Let's be serious. Do I look like a pious churchgoer? Or does Don Nicolo Vincenzo here? Not in the slightest! You see... we are a little – what can I say? – we've had a bit of an education, we read the gazettes and that's why we became liberals. What does that mean, eh? What does it mean? It means that we are against the Bourbons and their hangers-on, but we are also against the Church, which has fostered wrongs and stood by tyrants. As far as priests go... I can assure you that they're not all the same. You know Monsignor Adorno, Father Morelli of San Pantaleo, Father Artale of Saint Michele, the monks in the monastery, and every one of them is a friend and accomplice of the usurpers. But this Father Saccone of the Holy Rosary church, I can assure you that he's altogether different. First of all, his parish is poor. It doesn't have the land and rent of San Pantaleo or the Cathedral. Besides – and this must go no further – Father Saccone is a liberal. And then... he's a relation, a distant relation but still a relation, of a captain in Garibaldi's army. Who do you think has been giving me all this information about Garibaldi's men reaching Alcamo this morning and, we hope, Palermo by tomorrow? Can I tell you something else? If we do not win the support of these soldiers and liberals, who is going to proclaim to the world tomorrow that what we did was right? You follow? Now, Father Saccone happens to have a foible for oaths and vows. He says that it was always thus in all human memory, that those who accomplished the heroic deeds celebrated in history always sealed their pact with a solemn oath on the Bible: the assassins of Julius Caesar, the crusaders, the paladins of France, the Sicilian Vespers, the Battle of Legnano, the Great Oath of Pontida, the Challenge of Barletta... Father Saccone is a learned man, and he knows these things. And so? What are we to do? Anyway, are we not all devoted to Saint Nicolas? And what does Saint Nicolas hold in his hand? A book, a Bible. For a start, you yourself, Malandro, are you not one of the statue-bearers on the feast of the patron saint? And you, and you, and...' Don Ignazio pointed to each one in turn.

'Saint Nicolas is different,' murmured Turi Malandro.

'Come, my friends, let's not waste too much time on this nonsense... Father Saccone wants an oath on his Bible? Well then, why don't we swear? What does it matter to us? Bear in mind that once our women know that there's a priest involved, it'll be easier to coax them along. It's also worthwhile thinking about what will happen afterwards. Men of Alcara, I put it to you. Do you wish to swear the oath?'

'Yes,' the assembly replied as one.

'Glory to Saint Nicolas! Tonight, then, in front of the church of the Holy Rosary.'

Turi Malandro pulled his beret further down over his eyes, tugged at the reins of his mule which promptly turned round, showing its arse to all those present, and the two set off on their way back to the village. The horses of Don Ignazio and Don Nicolo Vincenzo too moved off in the same direction.

The shepherds and labourers took up their conversation, in the same strident tones, in threes in fours in fives, in the same groups as before. Then, some to the left and some to the right, they all tramped downhill towards the village.

Peppe Sirna, hoe over his shoulder, went with Bellicchia, Vinci, Quagliata, Misterio, Tanticchia and Tramontana. They walked in silence, in single file, jumping over obstacles, like Tanticchia's three she-goats. The goats ambled off up the slope now and again to snatch some leaves, displaying the practised finesse of light-fingered thieves, and then rushed downhill to munch at any broad-bean flower sticking out through the hedge. The billy goat followed after.

'Bruhunci,' called out Misterio, 'Rossa, Signorina, oh damn!' he said, throwing stones at them.

Carcagnintra was murmuring, making a speech to someone or other, with accompanying gestures and strange half words, in which all that was clear was the swearing – bugger this! bugger that!

Every so often, Quagliata, like a chorus, broke out with: 'My little piglets in their sty are as hungry as wolves. For four full days they've seen no swill.' And he laughed heartily, under his moustache, shaking his head from side to side.

Santo Misterio, famous for his songs and serenades, began to sing:

> To arms, to arms, the tocsin sounds,
> The Turks are at the gate.
> With sword and dagger, bullet, gun,
> We're masters of our fate.
>
> Come out, come out for freedom's sake,
> Rip out the guardsman's heart.
> So come now, boys, with sharpened blade
> Display the dagger's fearful art.
>
> For freedom's what the people want!
> Long live Sicilian liberty!

All over the countryside, in the Hermitage, at the Rogato, at the Holy Office, on the hilltops, in the valleys and at the gates of the towns, the vigil fires – lights, embers, signs, flaming hearts giving off sparks – were burning.

They arrived at the church of the Capuchins, passed by Mandrazza, crossed the bridge over the Stella (the evening breeze enveloped the swaying poplars in a strange music). They stopped, as was their custom, at the Abate square. The fountain was white, white in the surrounding night, with seven pipes at the base of a façade as beautiful as that of any church, splashing fresh water into the basin below. The basin, decorated with spirals, pinnacles, stone curlicues and miniature columns, seemed to swell out and curve back (a thorn-hedge with the yellow flowers of the unripe prickly pear was just visible). In the centre a crowned eagle was carved, with outstretched wings and fan tail; and beneath that, a grotesque face with puffed out cheeks, blowing on the waters. The men refreshed themselves. They took the Donadei road, and as they neared the end, in the narrow lane leading on to the piazza, at the corner beside the Club, they heard one of its middle-class members in the doorway, thumbs planted in waistcoat pocket, straw hat askew, sniff the air and assert sneeringly and offensively:

'Ah, what a scent of shit in the air this evening!'

They all stopped, she-goats and billy goat as well as humans, red with the rush of blood to the head. They looked at each other questioningly. Carcagnintra gripped the handle of the sickle in his belt. Sirna, with a swift movement of his shoulder, pulled forward the hoe that was slung over his back and held it before him as though issuing an 'on your guard'. Tanticchia drew from his sack a pair of sharp goat-shears. Patroniti, with one bound, placed himself behind them all, opened wide his arms and began to push, his chest against their backs, to move them on.

'Calmly does it, lads, calmly, keep your temper,' he kept repeating quietly, 'patience... patience, until tomorrow.'

They walked on, shoulder to shoulder, eyes forward, spines as rigid as a stone or papier-mâché statue, feet in rough patchwork or sheepskin footwear dragged heavily, their teeth clenched, breathing forced through the nose from barely restrained fury and bile.

'Ha, ha, scent of shit, papa, ha, ha', they heard once more from behind them, from Salvatorino – a boy as plump as a woman, a hare-brained mummy's pet, still sucking his thumb at fifteen years, nose running and mouth dribbling, son and heir, treasure and delight, light of the life of his father, the mayor Professor Ignazio, and of his grandfather, Bartolo the notary.

Taranticchia swivelled his head on his shoulders and glowered at him menacingly.

'Little pansy, son of a pansy college boy,' he shouted, and spat, white and hard, round as a coin, on the ground.

SIX

Letter of Enrico Pirajno, to the Advocate Giovanni Interdonato, as Preamble to a Petition on the Events at Alcara Li Fusi

Cefalu, 9 October 1860

Illustrious Interdonato, my friend,

Be good enough to cast your mind back to an evening in November 1856, when, in the company of a young man by the name of Palamara, you disembarked at Cefalu from a sailing ship from the Aeolian islands. You did me the honour of choosing me as your host and as the recipient of a gift, offered as a token of friendship and esteem, from yourself and the apothecary Carnevale. The object in question was a Greek earthenware statue, sculpted in Lipari, representing Kore, which I, thoughtlessly and with a foolish rhetorical flourish, named *Italia*. In order that you may from the outset be aware of the identity of the man who has the temerity to seek to distract you from the exercise of your public duties and offices, and may thus, without regret or remorse, feel free to set aside the present missive, Enrico Pirajno – the title 'of Mandralisca' is here added only to avoid confusion – declares himself the writer of this petition which he would like so submit for your perusal and reflection. He begs pardon for this preamble, for the prolixity of the document and for any defects of form or substance it may contain. Further, in order that without more delay your attention be drawn not only to the identity of the present writer – a trifling matter, of no consequence – but also to the subject of the present document, know that it deals with the atrocious events that occurred in Alcara Li Fusi, above the Nebrodi Mountains, in Val Demone, on 17 May and immediately thereafter. The present writer, alas! found himself, through the exercise of chance or destiny, spectator of some of these events. The same destiny or chance brings these events to the attention, and within the competence, of the High Court of Messina where you sit as Procurator General, having, as I learn from the Official Gazette, resigned as Minister for the Interior in Garibaldi's Government.

As we await the judgement which the said Court will in due course hand down on those of the accused – a group of peasants and shepherds from Alcara, some in custody and others still at large – who escaped the sentence of death by firing squad imposed by the Special Commission in Patti on 18 August, this petition must not be seen as a prejudicial plea to tilt the sacred scales of justice one way or the other, but is proffered as an independent, frank and objective means of imparting knowledge on acts committed by certain parties who have the misfortune not to possess (in addition to everything else) the necessary command of narrative in its spoken or written form, a privilege which I who now write, and which you, Interdonato, and the prosecution, the judiciary and counsel retained by injured parties all enjoy. What has History been until now, my illustrious friend? Unfailingly, a record of the privileged, written by the privileged. I was driven to this conclusion by my participation in the events in question.

At this point, I invoke the Supreme Being, Intellect or Reason or Whoever watches over us, to keep my mind clear and unclouded, and my memory sharp as I strive to narrate the course of those events.

Since there are already (and the volume will surely increase) an unconscionable number of addresses, essays, articles in reviews and pamphlets all hostile to the accused, it is my wish to narrate these events as they would have been narrated by one of the leaders of the uprising executed in Patti. Not perhaps Don Ignazio Cozzo, a member of the upper classes and thus skilled in speech and composition, but an illiterate farmhand, like Peppe Sirna known as Papa, the youngest and most innocent of the group. Will such a switch of voice and persona be possible, my friend? No, never! However willing the mind and heart may be, by reason of culture, birth or our estate we harbour within our very being too many voices, distortions, flaws. The writings of *soi-disant* enlightened spirits like us represent on every occasion a perhaps greater imposture than the approach of those blinded by obtuseness, by the privilege of class or the passions of caste. You will object: are there not statements, eye-witness accounts, declarations in the official records? Yes, but who writes down those words, who shapes those voices, who freezes them in the codices, who imposes on them the laws of language? A scribe, a transcriber, a clerk. What is needed is some imaginary mechanical device capable of capturing that speech in its raw state, just as the daguerreotype catches a likeness. And yet, even such an operation would be, if anything, even more unjust, since we lack the key, the code needed to interpret that speech.

At this point, it might be worthwhile to recall an incident that occurred to me. In the castle of the Granza Maniforti, in the village of Sant'Agata, I heard a prisoner declaim his outrage in his own tongue, the speech of San Fratello, a beautiful Romance or middle-Latin language which has remained intact for a thousand years but which is utterly incomprehensible to me and to all those who employ a modern vernacular code. Apart from the language, do we have in our possession the key, do we have access to the ciphers of being, of feeling and of resentment of these people? We hold unquestioningly to our own code, to that style of being and speech which has been given predominance over all others – the code of property and possession, the political code of the much-vaunted liberty and unity of Italy, the code of heroism of such as General Garibaldi and his followers, the code of poetry and science, the code of justice and of some sublime, unglimpsed utopia . . . And so we utter words like Revolution, Liberty, Equality, Democracy; with these words we fill gazettes, papers, books, plaques, treatises, constitutions . . . we who have already attained and possess those values, even if we have also seen them destroyed or threatened by the Tyrant or the Emperor, by Austria or the

Bourbons. But what of those others who have never attained the most sacred and elementary rights – bread and land, health and love, peace, joy and education – what obligation is there on such people (and they are the majority) to understand these words as we do?(The time will come when they will by their own efforts conquer such values, and then they will call them by new words, true for them and of necessity true for us too, true because the names will perfectly match the reality.]

What then is the worth of talk and writing, my friend? The wisest course of action for us would be to cast aside ink, inkwell and quill, to bury them in the ground, to end all chatter, to cease deceiving ourselves and others with the husks and slobber of snails and slugs, cochleas and helices, mud disguised as silver, white light, contorted beings, coils, unending circles, leatherlike clouds, baroque curls, slime and spittal, sticky stripes on the earth...

I once saw a snail mark out its trail in the form of a spiral, moving from the outside to the innermost point of no exit, as though repeating on the ground, in enlarged form, the design on its casing, the dark dungeon of its shell. And sitting there watching, I remembered with utter dismay all the various dead points, the vices, obsessions, manias, restrictions, destinies, decay, tombs, prisons... I recalled the different types of negation of all life, all escape, liberty and fantasy, of all eternal, unending creativity...

Snails, those beautiful hermaphrodite creatures, are worse than crows or jackals. They shun the sun, they wreak havoc on nursery-gardens and seeded fields, they draw their own nourishment from putrid liquids, from the fluid of corpses, from decomposing matter, they crawl into carcasses, suck the marrow of bones, search out the brain in the skull, the watery pupil in the eye-socket... it was not by chance that the Romans ate them at funeral feasts...

I confess: after the events of Alcara, I said goodbye to my insane idea of completing a study of the general terrestrial and fluvial malacology of Sicily. I set fire to my papers, to precious, rare books, I threw my microscope over the balcony wall, I crushed underfoot collected exemplars of each species and genus: *Ancylus, vitrina, helix, pupa, clausilia, bulinus, auricula*... To hell with them! (The joy and pleasure of hearing those husks crunched under my feet!)

What more, what is to be done, Interdonato my friend?

'Action, action!' some might urge on me. But for whom? With whom? And how? For Italy and the House of Savoy? With Garibaldi? By warfare?

I took part in the '56 uprising in Cefalu, which was uncovered then put down. I shared the exhilaration and hesitations of that handful of intrepid spirits, the Botta brothers, Guarnera, Maggio, Maranto, Sapienza, Bevilacqua, and of the standard-bearer your dear friend Giovannino Palamara. They attacked the guard post, disarmed the guards, then marched off to free Spinuzza from his chains... I saw them imprisoned, each one of them, together with the Botta girls and their aged mother, whose gentle hands had embroidered the golden threads of hope in the banner carried as symbol of a faith. I saw the soldiers' bullets shatter the breast of poor Spinuzza, impassive and proud, as fair as a Manfredi of Swabian descent... 'Offer your life to God, and then no executioner can ever boast of having taken it,' suggested the crow-like priest, Restivo, giving him the crucifix to kiss. Courageous to the last, he rejected the counsel and the signs of the Passion. 'I offer my life to Italy,' he replied. In the silence which followed the gunfire, the piercing, inhuman scream of the mad woman, Giovanna Oddo, fiancée of the newly dead man, rang through the air from a nearby balcony.

I said to myself then, before the dreadful, bloody events of Alcara, which I am about to relate once I have completed this preamble, I said to myself then – everything is good, everything is holy. There is justice in the death of Spinuzza, Bentivegna, Pisacane, who died as heroes, martyrs for an ideal, believers in a noble, ardent cause.

Today, I say: what is this belief, this ideal? An abstraction, a distraction, a yearning, an incorporeal flower, an ornamentation, a will o'the wisp... A snail. Because, for anyone who looks beneath – beneath the snail I mean – there is land – real, material, eternal land.

Ah the land! It was for that alone that the people in Alcara, in Biancavilla, Bronte, rose up, never for the snails.

Action then, Interdonato? No, no, not for me. The only worthwhile action I plan to undertake is to leave my house and property and have it converted to provide education and tuition for the children of the ordinary people of my home town of Cefalu. It is my hope that they will one day write their history, or rather that they will write history, by themselves, rather than entrust the task to me or to you, Interdonato, or to some hired clerk, all of us by birth, by rank or disposition too prone to add frills and flourishes, airy spirals, labyrinths... snails. The books, the classical collection and the paintings will form the basis of a public library and museum, in which, as you already know, the centrepiece, sparkling like a jewel, will be Antonello's portrait of that Unknown Man, who has such an uncanny resemblance to you... and perhaps – a little – to me too, to my cousin Bordonaro, to the painter Bevelacqua, to the bishop of this place, Ruggiero Blundo, and even – it distresses me to have to say – to the former Bourbon minister, Cassisi, and to the Police director, Maniscalco... Do you wish to know something else? By staring for long periods at that unnamed man, here in my studio, opposite my desk, I have come to understand why your fiancée, Catena Carnevale, took a knife to it at exactly the point where the lip barely puckers into that faint, ironic, mordant smile, into that smile which is the flower of intelligence, of reason and wisdom but also of detachment, of distance (like the physical distancing you once suffered, forced to wander through the seas, ports and capitals of Europe and Africa), of the aristocracy of birth, of wealth, of culture, of power deriving from office...

I have come to understand: a snail! That smile too is a snail!

Action, I was saying, Interdonato. It is now your turn, my good friend. It is your turn to act, and not in the name of the Ideal, but of an authentic, concrete cause; by chance or the design of fate, you, in your capacity as Procurator General of the High Court of Messina, find yourself in a position to decide on the life or death of men who acted with violence – there can be no denial – but who were goaded by an even greater violence inflicted by others over the centuries, by the experience of oppression, injustice, deception.

Permit me to quote here this reflection by Mario Pagano.

'Thus it is, mortal man, that if you extend your hand and your reach beyond the limits afforded you by nature, if you seize for yourself the products of the earth, offending your fellow man and denying him the means of survival, you will feel the force of his wrath. Your crime is the invasion and violation of order; your penalty will be your own destruction.' This though was reiterated by Pisacane, who commented: 'The guarantee of the enjoyment of the fruit of one's own labour; all other property not only abolished but suppressed by law as theft – these must be the keystones of the new social structure. It is now time to execute the solemn sentence which Nature pronounced through the mouth of Mario Pagano: the destruction of usurpers.'

Property, Interdonato, the most crass, monstrous, all-devouring snail ever to make its way in this world. It was to destroy it that the citizens of Alçara rose up. They were stirred by a real, concrete, corporal cause – land, the deepest point, navel, tomb and regeneration, life and death, winter and spring, Hades and Demeter, Kore bearing gifts in her arms, the cornsheaf, the sweet pomegranate...

SEVEN

The Petition

Cefalu, 15 October 1860.

I spoke in the above preamble of a petition, of an account of those events, which, in recent days, depriving myself of sleep and rest, I have made every effort to draw up. But on every occasion my inability to find an opening, a style and a tone, to find the words and the arrangement of words appropriate for the description of these happenings has caused the pen to drop from my hand. My embarrassment and shame have increased with my failure to conceive an order or a form resemble in imagination the boundaries of a time and a space which might contain that explosion, that startling peal of trumpets, that awesome cyclone. And the roots, the reasons, the deep, remote discontents in which these events had their origin? And lastly, the contradiction of finding myself talking, as I have talked, of the impossibility of writing if one is to avoid betrayal and imposture, and at the same time of the need and urge to write.

It was easy, and indeed permissible, for me to discuss only the outcome of the events and the actions which followed the uprising, not least because I had witnessed them. In the aftermath the leaders, who had been at liberty for the previous thirty days to do and undo at will, to implement those expropriations and killings which have caused such dismay on all sides, felt the full brunt of public indignation, in deeds and words.

Thus the pen dropped from my hand.

But here in my study – a flash of lightning – in the course of the night just past (the laughter of the Unknown Mariner, in the shadowy light, altered from the light-hearted and ironical to the severe, sardonic and malicious), I recalled some papers on which I had, with all the scrupulous fidelity of a notary, taken down in my own hand charcoal scrawls which had been written on a wall as though by some mechanical device, by a detached hand, independent of mind and body. They were the personal testimony of certain of the leaders, some of whom later met their death before a firing squad – of, I imagine, Don Ignazio Cozzo, of Peppe Sirna, Turi Malandro, Michele Patroniti and others again.

Where had I found those writings? And who had shaped, who had given being to those passionate voices?

In order to explain I must delve back into the past.

On 16 May, intent on pursuing that foolish, damnable scheme of mine to research and catalogue the snails of Sicily, I arrived in Alcara as the guest of Baron Crescenzio Manca. The following day, the feast of the Ascension, rioting broke out in the streets of the town, but having been forewarned by an emissary of a certain Father Saccone, parish priest in the Church of the Holy Rosary, we fled through the rocky countryside near by to the slopes of Calanna where, under the protection of a mad hermit, we took refuge in the Hermitage of San Nicolo. This black, deranged moon-calf, waving his staff threateningly in the air, would waken us all, women and trembling, tearful children included, in the middle of the night and oblige us to prostrate ourselves and expiate sin by kissing a basket containing a mantle, a tiny shoe, a lock of hair – all relics, as far as I could gather from his ravings, belonging to a holy virgin who had died, risen again and then died a second time through the grace of the cross. We were then constrained to implore in turn the aid of demons and of celestial spirits. After some forty-eight hours of this terrifying existence, which would have killed us off or driven us insane had it continued (my serving man, Rosario, was reduced to a state of virtual slavery or drivelling dependency on the friar, and in his delirium the idiot came to worship him, to permit himself to be beaten, to be dressed in a hair shirt and even to have dust and excrement smeared over his head), we heard that the rising was at an end and we were liberated.

Astride donkeys, horses and mules, and even on the backs of the Baron's loyal, faithful servants, we made slow progress across the arid stones and slopes of Calanna, away from captivity in the hermitage of that insane werewolf of a friar towards the town, broken and ill, I in body from sheer exhaustion, my servant in mind from sheer fatuity.

In front of the Pietrami peak, on the Vignazza road, which leads via Serra di Re and Maniace to Bronte, we met the first human beings we had seen, two field guards. To their evident rage, they were finding it difficult to get up the hill and, swearing loudly, were pricking their donkeys' buttocks to blood with their goads.

'Hallo, hallo!' we shouted, 'good people, guards, what news from Alcara?'

'Dreadful news,' they replied, and continued on their way, cursing.

The 24th of June, five o'clock in the afternoon.

The first station was at Paratica, on the square in front of the Capuchin monastery.

Will I ever be able to describe that theatre, that fearful sight which presented itself to my eyes in the streets and squares of the town? Nothing less would be sufficient than the genius of Dante, the fervour of Alfieri, the verve of Foscolo or Byron, the expansive prose of D'Azeglio, Victor Hugo or Guerrazzi, or that fire and flaming dagger, endowed with the power to melt ink frozen from very horror on the tip of the pen, possessed by the English tragedian, the Britannic angel. Will you be contented with me to whom Nature, alas! has allotted no more than aspiration, frailty and anguish.

In any case: at the first station, the spectacle consists of hosts of the ancient, embalmed dead scattered in the open air, monks and patricians ripped from fresh tombs and catacombs, exposed to the irreverence of midday suns, of moons, rains, morning dews. In their tattered finery, mildewed damasks and faded silks, one laughs, another weeps and another screams. On one side, a shapeless bundle of bones, ribs, skulls, femurs and forearms; on the other utensils, furnishings, sacks, wine-jars, barrels, bottles and demijohns. All around, ashes, cinders, charred wood, the smouldering embers of chests, chairs, cabinets, mattresses, bibles and parchments. The church, monastery and outhouses all lying open, gutted, deserted, sunk in mournful silence. Only one faint,

weary, extended wail, a falsetto note such as a poor actor or nar-
rator might make, vibrated in the air. Its source, not easy to trace,
seemed to be moving, now high in the bell tower or cypress tree,
now sealed in a giant pitcher, in a well, in a sarcophagus or underground cellar. Was it some friar walled up, as occurred in *She's
Buried Alive*, or some spirit associated with the place?

Second station: the Abate square.

At the fountain of perpetual song from the seven fresh mouths
of clear water, even the donkeys turned away their heads, as did
the mules, notoriously fastidious by nature, as did the servants
and indeed all present. A heavy, unclean stench of swollen carcasses on the surface of the water, a slaughterhouse of hindquarters,
bellies, lungs and intestines, impossible to identify as belonging
to cattle, goats, pigs, dogs or humans, lying in the sodden earth
and in pools of water. The same sight at the wash-house a little
lower down, with wheels, cannon-balls, white limestone columns scattered around pell-mell. From the mill up above, from
Castle Turio, from Holy Trinity, columns of solid, dark smoke
spiralled upwards, dispersed overhead and, in the still air of a June
midday, created black vortices or surges and eddies, as black as
the flocks of crows that hovered over the fig trees, walls and
thorn-hedges, or formed figures while they circled furiously in
the sky.

And third station: the square of the church dedicated to Saint
Nicolas, the heart of the town, site of the Cathedral, the Nobles'
Club, the grain store, the Archive, the portals and circular bal-
conies of the palaces and grand residences of the affluent.

On every side, devastation: mist, ashes, earth, wind and
smoke.

Che passa? Some apocalyptic force has passed this way.

In the warm, desolate piazza, corpses which had died dreadful
deaths were lying, decomposing, in the doorway of the Club,
while the bodies of boys, of young and old men were piled one
on top of the other on the flagstones in front. Trampled to death,
stabbed, lying in the squalid filth of dried alcohol, wine dregs,
secretions, stains, torn flesh, in the stench of rank fermentations,
of acids, of putrefying yeasts, of rotting eggs and mouldering
cheeses. Swarms of buzzing dung beetles, flies, mosquitoes.

It was midday, midday without end.

All is topsy turvy. One can't look.

With a sudden swoop, crows, jackdaws, ravens glide down from the heights of the beetling crags, Bruno and Minnivacche, to land on the angels, the cross, the weathervane, the national banner, the wheel-hubs, the pivots and breech pieces. Stray dogs, terriers, bloodhounds and mangy mongrels roam around. Herds of pigs too, free of rope and halter, mad with freedom, inebriated with the filth they wallow in, as black and wild as boars.

What more can one do?

The vulture can do more. A wing-span covering more than three metres, claws tense, talons curved, its vast, bloated bulk plummeted as though falling from the empyrean. The Carnivorous Vulture settled on the decomposing dead; it sunk its beak into the cadaver, dug deep, gave a vigorous tug with the head and extracted a morsel from the belly or throat. It pulled itself upright, and flew off with a wild screech.

This is how it happened.

I remain silent on the other acts of plunder and destruction: of the archives, furnishings and registers of the Town Hall, some burned and others scattered pell-mell; of the statues of the Mother of God, of the Virgins, Doctors and Patriarchs, the votive offerings, glass cases enclosing the Infant Jesus, the woods, stuccos, waxes, papier mâchés, the drapes, veils, tarlatan bouquets, vestments of Father Adorno, the archpriest, all scattered in confusion in front of the church.

I remain silent too on the other churches, on the nuns raped in cloisters, in houses, in the streets and squares of the city.

Down one of those streets, Via Donodei, I saw an old woman walk barefoot, head uncovered, her white hair flowing freely over her shoulders. With one hand she gripped a finely made, grand drum and with the other she caressed the taut skin slowly, warming it with a circular movement. A little boy, hugging in his arms a handleless clay vessel, a jug or a pitcher, bounded nimbly along after her. From the mouth of the vase, tender, clear green shoots bearing the first barley, wheat or chick pea buds emerged robustly. Having made their way across the piazza (the boy held his nose with his fingers), the two entered the Cathedral and placed the pitcher on the altar. The woman began to beat the drum. The 24th of June was in Alcara the feast of the Pitcher, and it was the custom in that district to celebrate those vessels and shrubs with singing and dancing until well into the night. Enemies were then reconciled, marriages arranged, godparents chosen.

Strange devotion.

All of a sudden, the bells of the north-facing church began to ring out. The rattle of shots, explosions, muffled blows, cries, shouts, the sound of running feet were carried down from somewhere up above.

What is this hubbub?

A group of men in the grip of fury and panic came running from the Motta district of the town. 'Treachery! Help! Treachery!' they shouted as they ran, clanging their sheep bells, still gripping their pitchforks, rifles, axes, scythes, fleeing towards Mandrazza, the Palo, and further off towards Bacco, Lemena and the Rogato.

And then, from up above, from down below, the tocsin sounded, bells from the churches of the Annunciation, the Holy Rosary, Blessed Grace rang out, filling the air with deep, sharp and median peals, according to the secret arts of the foundries of Tortorici.

And now it is the time of lamentations, of bitter weeping, of mourning. Mothers, sisters, wives in closely clinging groups, black huddles of shawls and veils, appear as though by enchantment near the piled bodies, their heads and shoulders swaying to the cadences of the slow music. The first solo is that of a woman who invokes, with piercing head voice, her son whose throat was slashed open.

Unhappy mother.

'Oh Turuzzo, Turi, Tu!'

The chorus echoes the words, in reverse order.

'Tu, Turi, Turuzzo, Oh!'

And then her husband, Gnazio, and the notary, her father-in-law. Other women's voices are heard, calling for Peppe, calling for Luigi, Vicenzo, Ciccio, Tano, Pasqualino...

Appeals are in vain.

In the meantime, a coach, drawn by the skeleton of a mule, similar to the gaunt beast which gallops over the heads of popes and princes in Palazzo Sclafani in Palermo, came on the scene. A strange coachman, with red shirt, wearing a handkerchief round his neck and a military cap with visor, standing erect on the wagon, clasping reins and whip, yelled in rasping tones:

'Move, move, you filthy beast, move you Moroccan bastard . . . like the rest of this lot.'

Three others dressed like the first, taking position alongside the coach, break into sniggers. Holding sabres, rifles and revolvers they have a group of Alcaresi in custody. Who are they? They are the soldiers from the north who landed with Garibaldi to free us from the Bourbon yoke.

Yes, they are of another breed.

The convoy comes to a halt in front of the bodies, and the soldiers then make the townspeople load the dead onto the cart. The screams of the women become more shrill, the night-owls in the bell tower take flight. They throw a watered-yellow altar cloth over the shifting load, not quite covering protruding heads, legs, hands.

Cartloads for the cemetery.

It is seven in the evening, shadows lengthen on the ground, and the sun sets on the sea.

Under the full moon, a solitary coachman carried his cargo of salt into the mountains, where he was caught by a storm . . .

The revolt was put down by trickery. Who was responsible for the deception? A colonel. He said:

'I have been sent by the General.'

'Long live Garibaldi,' came the answering cry.

'Brave men, brave patriots!' replied the colonel, and went on: 'Your merits are great. The Dictator of Sicily will reward you. But now, lay down your arms, hand them over to my soldiers.'

And there and then, he arrested forty of them.

'Truth is dead, a bitter fate is ours,' cried Turi Malandro, like a damned soul. Don Nicolo Vincenzo began to weep.

To the sound of trumpets, wooden clogs and irons, they came into the piazza, the colonel at the head, bold and fearless in the saddle.

'Savages! beasts!' he proclaimed, at the sight of the devastated houses, of the still smouldering fires, of the barricades, and at the lingering smell of the hardened blood and gore on the paving.

'Quicklime, at once,' cried the commander, 'otherwise we'll all be dead of cholera.'

With basins, jugs and scrubbing brushes, they washed the flagstones, pedestals, walls, doors, portals and architraves.

At seven o'clock, as evening drew in, they lit the gas mantles in the glass cased lamp posts. And the candles and oil lamps which had been left on the altar. The organ struck up and boomed out, as Father Adorno intoned:

Te Deum laudamus . . .

The weeping fell away, the jubilation swelled up through the nave.

From the altar steps, our colonel, in full dress uniform with tassels and golds, with silver sabre and ceremonial, damask steel rifle criss-crossed over his back, harangued us nobles:

'Citizens of Alcara, take comfort, the terror is at an end. Those who are lined up in chains outside are not men but bestial furies, jackals who took advantage of the sacred name of our leader Garibaldi, of King Victor Emmanuel and of Italy to carry out massacre, plunder and theft. Here in the sight of God, I declare those rebels guilty of a crime against humanity. And I give you my word as colonel that those shameless Bourbon lackeys who have sullied our tricolour with blood will pay for their nefarious offences.'

Weeping and murmuring once more from the nave.

'But be of good heart,' continued the colonel, 'the dawn of liberty is still ours and it is already day. A new struggle awaits us at the castle of Milazzo. In a matter of hours, Brigadier Medici's column, some of whose vanguard you saw a little while ago on the piazza, is expected in Barcellona. Meanwhile, by the authority conferred on me by Doctor Pancaldo, Governor of the province of Messina, I confer on you, Don Luigi Bartolo Gentile, the powers of Mayor of the Council, and I invite you all to root out and proceed to the arrest of all the other criminals who have so far evaded capture. Those murderers who are in our hands will be this very evening transported to the prison in the Granza Maniforti castle in Sant'Agata, and from there to Patti, to be tried by a Special Commission. Italy United and Free will not tolerate a rabble in its midst. Long live Italy, long live Garibaldi, long live the noble soldier king! Viva Vittorio Emmanuele!'

'Viva, viva Vittorio Emmanuele!' replied the Alcaresi in unison.

The colonel came down from the altar and crossed the church, his spurs jingling as he walked, his binoculars dancing on his chest, as erect and proud as a Washington, and on the doorway, the present writer, I myself, stepped in front of him.

'I am Enrico Pirajno, from Cefalu. Are you from Sicily, colonel?'

'From Sicily, yes. Roccalumera, to be precise.' And immediately he added, after looking me up and down.

'I know you, Mandralisca. The Botta brothers and Andrea Maggio in the prison at Favignana spoke about you. But, you... here, what are you here for?'

'Snails...I am here for snails. Forgive me, colonel. You are...?'

'Giovanni Interdonato.'

'No!'

'Yes!'

'Forgive me. It's just that I once knew another Interdonato...'

'My cousin, the lawyer, to whom you once afforded hospitality while he was in hiding. He resembles me only in name, for the rest we differ...'

'Where is he now?'

'In Palermo. He has just been named Minister for the Interior in this first Dictatorial Government. But is there some service I can do you, Baron?'

'Help me to get as soon as possible to the castle of Prince Galvano Granza Maniforti...'

'A great patriot who has served the cause well! I will do as you request.'

And with these words, he continued on his fated way.

However, I was constrained, Interdonato, to remain another week or more in that town, since there were no horses or coaches, and since the mayor issued an order that everyone, excepting the Guards, was to stay indoors, that no one was to enter or leave the town which had seen itself reduced to the condition of cursed land, quarantine, besieged city or daytime curfew. By day, then, the rooms echoed to pursuits, to galloping hooves, peeling bells, gunfire, appeals, orders, shouts, halts, yells, trumpet blasts, and all these things which by day were real and decipherable, by night were made by night confused, agonising, terrifying...

Yes, it is time to flee, to seek concealment. It is time to wait, wait in stillness, in immobility, as though turned to rock. In the hysteria of night, the sounding trumpets advance in circles, in ellipses, in encircling waves. Let the very sound of breathing die away. The fierce, iron bugles, the flocks of dark cherubim graze the parabola – the curve pulls apart the fibres – they decline, fade at the parabola's horns. And here, in this mildewing corner...

Let them come, let them come, those iron-rattling hordes, with their screaming sirens and night blades, for the gnaw of silence, of stillness is yet more remorseless.

But you must wait, tread softly. Away with your hauteur, your show of rank, the senseless games of passing days. Leave misery to flow in its own sewers, focus your mind. Be a man for a moment. Place your foot here, on this earth, enter in, gaze at the scene: in this little space invaded by the night, you will find the passageways, the exits, and flee, flee if you can from the curse of guilt. Listen: to the awesome death rattle emitted by a body glimpsed in a perspective worthy of Mantegna. The man hurled from the window fell on shards of crystal.

> Death! What makes you rush this day
> To pluck carnations in full bloom?

They throw up barriers, walls, labyrinths. And from the stones of the strong, the snailshell of terror, the gentle madman immured alive (they stopped the foot which fashioned odd, free spirals in the air) screams in the night. This slow agony is already death... And the cry ricochets from house to house, from porphyry staircases, damask screens, against high-backed chairs, podiums, glass cases.

'Will someone stop his mouth!' they cry, raising over their heads mantles, copes, cloaks, ermine capes.

Do not be taken in by the feverish light surrounding the diaphanous cleric. The garb covers sores, wounds, filth, conceit. Schizophrenia conceals from him the flow of events, conditions imposed on others. This man is a stranger in the home of his chicks.

In underground coops, between arsenic fumes and draining cyanide, for my and your good, they are pecking at the empty, round, dilated unseeing eye, they are cutting veins, tendons, muscles. In a cycle of bran and shit, bran and shit.

Touch your stomach now, from sternum to navel, with unwavering fingers; do you feel the mark of your severed belly, the cut for the escape of bile? And here, where are the escape chutes? For all the imbalance, dissonance, distortion, I refuse you your bran and my shit, you who are of the race of the angels!

But at the dead of night, the hordes are already battering at the door, hauling at the locks and hinges, kicking with nailed boots, leaving chalked crosses on the doorways and lintels.

The rebel emerges, seize him! Secure him with chains and handcuffs, bind his neck with gorse cord.

And in the immense square, the drum falls silent and the captain shouts:

'Death by hanging, the body to be left three days on the gibbet!'

A heavy, hot scirocco wind blew up and howled like a wild beast on the hilltops and gorges, along the pavements and in the underground cells. Only then, preceded by a drummer marching through the deserted streets, did the town crier announce the lifting of the mayor's proclamation, leaving everyone free to come and go. In the morning, there was a knock at the door and Matafu, my friend Maniforti's servant, appeared to take us away (my own servant Rosario, who was regaining his wits, threw himself on his neck and kissed him repeatedly, as though he were his father returned from beyond the grave).

Twenty-four hours later, we were at the coast. In the castle I met up with my dear consort, in tears, who had arrived in the company of her cousin Bordonaro.

At the castle there was an encampment of the Alcara nobles,

Chiuppa, Capito, Versaci, Cortese, Frangipane, who had taken refuge there during the forty days of anarchy and were now making ready to return.

The time has now come, my dear Interdonato, when I can talk to you of the place where I found the famous writings, those charcoal documents which I read and transcribed from the walls of a secret pit under the castle which was being used as a prison. Prince Galvano was proud to have me visit the place where he had held the Alcara rebels for three days before they were taken to Patti for trial.

I must provide you with some outline of this castle.

EIGHT

The Prison

I cannot proceed until I have transcribed here, by way of epigraph, like a plaque in an entrance hall, this passage from a late eighteenth-century work entitled: *Re-creation of the Eye and Mind in the Observation of the Snail*, by Father Filippo Buonanni, a Jesuit priest.

> I am confident that you will not consider me guilty of hyperbole if, casting your glance solely on the coils on the surface of the snail's shell, you ponder the trouble geometricians have in designing it with precision. No matter how great the effort they dedicate to the task, the result is invariably disappointing, for they will have the shell composed of portions of circle of ever decreasing size, while the patterns are not circles, however circular they may appear.
>
> What Vitruvius fashioned for them so fanciful a home, and one so impossible to imitate in art? I make so bold as to say that with whatever zeal you search out causes, you will observe ever more forcibly that in each of His works God, in the guise of Nature, geometrises, as the Ancients would have it, so that His thoughts can be represented with equal pain, and pleasure, in the coils of a snail's shell.

'What is the relevance of snails here?' I hear you ask. They are relevant, my dear Interdonato. For the simple reason that the prison of which I am about to speak has the exact shape of the spirals of a snail's shell.

Having, so to speak, placed one of the legs of the compasses on this point, let us now position the other – but very briefly, to avoid boring you – on the origin and history of the castle which houses, below its foundations, this prison. It is named Sant'Agata, with the addition of the words 'of Militello', since as recently as 1857 it did not enjoy full municipal autonomy, but was governed from the other place. Its history is intimately linked with Militello in the Val Demone, in the district and diocese of Patti. Until 1600, it was no more than a fortress (the castle under discussion), but then, at an uncertain date, the surrounding territory was populated by a colony from the vicinity of Mount Etna who, driven either by hunger and famine or by earthquake and eruption, migrated from the interior towards the coast. This is proven by the dialect in use, by the occurrence of certain proper names typical of Catania, and most significantly by the decision of the village to adopt the name of the Virgin–Martyr who is patron saint of Catania. Indeed, in a niche in the arch over the road leading to the sea, one can still see a stone sculpture in which the Saint, holding open her tunic over a breast which is as flat as if Saint Joseph had passed his plane over it, shows passers-by her terrible mutilation, although whether in pride or pain it is impossible to ascertain. The display of her breast has led many to mistake her for Christ the Redeemer, who is often depicted with His hands in the same position.

On the south wall of the castle, this plaque has been affixed: TEMPORE DOMINI EXC. D. HIERONYMI (COCALI) GALLEGO PRINCIPIS MILITELLI AC MARCHIONIS SANCTAE AGATHAE, ANNO DOMINI MDCLXXV.

This Gallego family, natives of Galicia, as the name suggests, having been made by Philip IV Princes of Militello and Marquises of Sant'Agata, had the fortress built on the coast, while the Hieronymus/Girolamo (Cocalo), of the plaque, having married a Corbera, was, in my view, responsible for having it extended and transformed into a residential castle. He undoubtedly summoned a Spanish architect or geometrician to oversee the task, for only a Spanish mind could conceive of a mansion constructed in accordance with the pattern of a snail's shell, or *caracol* as they call it in their language. We are convinced that the unusual, fanciful name Cocalo enclosed in brackets after that of Girolamo, prince and marquis, must indicate an academician versed in the arts and sciences, for otherwise the choice of a pagan name would have led to condemnation for heresy. We are also convinced that the name must have provided the architect with his inspiration. Since Cocalo was the king of Sicily who welcomed Dedalus, the designer of the Labyrinth, after his flight through the skies from Crete and Minos, and since the name Cocalo contains in its derivation the ideal of snail's shell (*kochlias* in Greek, *cochlea* in Latin), there is the enigma resolved, the labyrinth shown to be fake. It had been equipped with a beginning and end, with an opening which is sunlit and a lower section which is closed and dark, with a great entrance from which one can also exit if one follows the winding but logical curve – as was the case with Pascal's snail – of its spiral. The architect constructed the castle according to this name: a homecoming after the great labyrinth without exit that is Spain, a secret dream of becoming one day Viceroy of Sicily, a creative gesture in defiance of Nature, like the wax wings of the Greek inventor, or simply whimsical fancy?

The strange fact is that the castle, having passed from the Gallego to the Maniforti family, has no grand, vertically rising staircases or simple stairways, nor does it have straight lines, corners, angles or square shapes; everything – stairs, stairwells, towers, courtyards and stores – is constructed of circles, hollows, curves and coild. And the most fantastic fantasy of all is displayed in that deep cellar, hypogeum, noria, contorted funnel, or convoluted sulphur pit, which is almost a mirror image or inverted model of the main body of the castle under which the prison is situated: an immense snail's shell with the opening on the top and the apex beneath, in the mud and filth.

From the courtyard, access to the castle is via a massive iron gate with close-fitted grating, wedged into the lumachella stone portal, which is itself a perfect arch lined with nine square, finely worked ashlars on either side, plus the keystone, various figures and bas-reliefs. Each of these is distinct, but each resembles or corresponds to its counterpart on the column opposite, with the keystone being unique, serving to divide and unite, to lock together the twin thrusts, the contraposed order of the resemblances.

Starting from ground level, moving from the left-hand pillar to the right, and from the first two lower ashlars upwards, the carvings portray: a geometric disposition of balls or apples and one of suns or moons rising or setting; a bunch of sunflowers in the midst of four leaves and two baskets of flowers in a cornucopia of plenty; a tuna fish and a dolphin; an artistic arrangement of knots resembling a necklace and two serpents entangled by the tail in the style of a caduceus; a winged she-dragon and a siren; a cock and a goose; a swan and a peacock; a harpy and a chimera; a seraph and an angel; and finally, in the centre, on the façade of the keystone, one word ringed by a corona, short but made indecipherable by the effect of centuries of rain, which, falling perpendicularly from a gargoyle above, has worn away the lettering.

Once the lock and chains were released, the bolt and bars pulled back, the grille undone, we found ourselves in the oval entranceway. Matafu went ahead with his lantern.

At once, the sounds of the sea, the low murmur and constant lapping of the waves rose from the depths, echo upon echo which, multiplying in their ascending, tortuous way up the shaft, dispersed on the ground and in the air of the courtyard, like the voice supposedly held captive in sea-shells. Those shells, splendid in form and colour, of the univalve or turbinate genus, and of the auriculae, buccina, galeiform, fluted or horned, umbilicus or scaragol and mytilus species, are all, when holed in the top, capable of use as triton or shell-trumpet (as it is commonly called), and employed by fishermen to attract fish or to call to each other in the vast sea of night. For this reason some were called in Antiquity Conchiliari or Conchiti, hence Plautus: *Salvete fures maritimi Conchitae, arque Namiotae, famelica hominum natio, quid agitis?*

And Virgil... but where was I? We were talking about the echoes. Our voices, whispers, breathing, Matafu's asthmatic wheeze, Granza Maniforti's sniggers, our footsteps, inflated beyond recognition, pursued us as we began to descend, following the circular path. We made our way down on cobblestones covered with layers of slippery moss and lichen, between tunnel walls and ceiling smoothed and shining with mortar or gesso, in some places seemingly coated with mother-of-pearl, crushed glass, Indian red paint or lacquer, with purple edgings shading into milk-white and pink tints in the inner sections, and all as bright as Chinese porcelain; in others, bulging and peeling with water dripping from the vaults to form calcified razor clams, tarnished by brown and green mildew or by the saltpetre and maidenhair fern which tumbled from the numerous cracks. A place of prime delights, a refuge of refreshment for the prince and the court during the three days of scorching scirocco, like the flowing waters of the Zisa, the lakes and streams of Maredolce, the gardens planted with bergamots and palm trees, the espaliers with jasmine stars, datura trumpets and magnolia curls, the kiosks and cubical pavilions of the Muslim caliphs; or like the wayward fantasies of gurgling waters and lush greenery, the riot of stones and shells devised by the architect Ligorio Pirro for Cardinal D'Este.

To all this life, farewell! Now a desolate desert, a purgatory, a pit of penitence and torture. Fetters, rings and chains at every turn, mattresses and covers pell-mell, encrusted chamber-pots, water pots, vessels and outsized cups, the odour of dried piss and, with respect, shit.

Hard by the bend from the vestibule, in the first curve where the light of the sun still shone, I saw the word Liberty on the wall, and by the flickering light of a smoky lantern I made out other freshly written words lower down, in the third and fifth curves and so on down to the lowest extremity where a concave stone formed the apex and closed off this pit (outside the sea surged against it, leaving the undertow ringing in our ears).

I made out that I had not seen anything. To put him off the track and break the silence, I asked Maniforti:

'That young prisoner from San Fratello, whatever became of him?'

'In Mistretta, in Mistretta, with an entirely reasonable sentence of three years in irons, on bread and water.'

With the complicity of Matafu, I returned to the prison the following day, equipped with pen, paper and ink, accompanied by my servant who held the lamp.

What I read I wrote down exactly as it was, and I here relay it to you, Interdonato. I enclose also an outline map, sketched on a plane surface, of that curving prison so that you can distinguish the exact location of all the graffiti in the spirals.

The spiral is arranged on coordinates on the model that takes its name from Archimedes, who left us the work *Peri Helicon*, that is *On Spirals*. These spirals are described as being on a plane, as though generated by one point moving at a uniform motion along a straight line, while the line itself rotates around one point. Therefore, setting our spiral on the orthogonals x and y, and proceeding from the internal terminal point (infinitesimal in theory, precisely as infinite are the sufferings, pains, torments, tears, terrors, poisons, despairs – but what can we know of them? what can we know of them? – trailed behind the people who here speak) towards the exterior, I have numbered every bend in the spiral. Each bend corresponds to the preceding one but is at the same time its continuation: at every half spiral or bend I have put a cardinal number, and each cardinal number represents a piece of writing.

Cochlias legere, to read shells, they used to say in Antiquity, referring to collections made on the beaches as an agreeable pastime or game.

But now we must *read this shell* as a matter of duty, with both bitterness and hope, in the sense that it is incumbent on us to interpret these signs on the walls, eloquent as they are of ancient sufferings and therefore of the impulse to strike back: to take cognizance of the history which comes swirling up from the depths; to imagine the history which will be created in days to come.

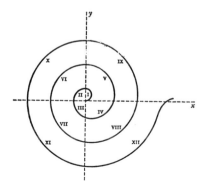

NINE

The Writings

I

HAVING SEEN
MY BROTHER SLAUGHTERED
WITH THREATENING WORDS
I ROBBED HIS WIFE AND WIDOW
I LAID WASTE THE VINES AND ORCHARD
I EMPTIED THE FAMILY'S HOME
OF ALL THE VICTUALS GOODS AND FURNISHINGS
WHICH OUR FATHER IN HIS WILL
LEFT TO HIM
HIS SWAGGERING FIRST-BORN SON.
NOW WHO KNOWS
MY DEAREST MOTHER
WHAT WILL BECOME OF ME

II

THE OWNERS OF THE FREEHOLD LANDS
THE BIGWIGS IN THE CITY HALLS
PARISH PRIESTS AND GENTLEMEN
SEIZED FOR THEMSELVES
THE COMMON LANDS
ALTHOUGH MYSELF A GENTLEMAN
WITH EQUAL RIGHTS TO THEIRS

I WAS LEFT EMPTY HANDED
LIKE THE POOREST PEASANTS
I URGED THE MEN OF ALCARA TO REVOLT
AH WRETCHED DAY
NONE COULD RESTRAIN THE FURY
OF THE UNLEASHED WOLVES
FAREWELL ALCARA
I BEG PARDON OF ALL MEN
FAREWELL WORLD

III

THE STENCH OF SHIT ON US
THE NIGHT WE FELL ON THE TOWN
I ROOTED OUT TURUZZO
GRANDSON OF THE NOTARY
DRAGGED HIM FROM HIS HOME
HELD HIM BETWEEN MY LEGS
AND SLIT HIS THROAT
HE WOULD HAVE BEEN A NOTARY ONE DAY

IV

THE WINTER WHEN FAMINE STRUCK
ONLY DEBTS TO FEED SEVEN MOUTHS
THEY BANISHED ME TO FLORESTA
DON IGNAZIO, PROFESSOR SON OF THE NOTARY
WRONGED MY DAUGHTER
WITH THESE HANDS I TORE
THAT WRETCH APART
AND STOPPED HIS MOUTH
WITH HIS OWN PRICK AND BALLS

V

I ATTACKED DON VINCENZO THE TAX-COLLECTOR
STABBED HIM
THREW HIS BODY TO THE PIGS
HE HAD ME BY THE THROAT WITH HIS BRIBES INTEREST ARREARS
HE STOLE THE STONEFREE LAND AT SCAVIOLI

VI

NEVER IN MY LIFE HAD I HANDLED
A RIFLE
AND YET THAT MORNING
I SHOT STRAIGHT
AGAINST THE JEWISH CLASS OF NOBLES
WHO KNOWS WHO I STRUCK
PERHAPS DON TANO THE TREASURER
OR PERHAPS MASTER CICCIO THE CIVIC COURIER

VII

VIVA L'ITALIA
CRIED THE GENTLEMAN
VENGEANCE VENGEANCE
JUSTICE
WAS OUR LEADER'S WORD
ON TO THAT GANG OF NOBLES AT ONCE
THIEVES AND EXPLOITERS
YOUNG LANZA CAME MY WAY
ALL SMILES
HE FELL IN A HEAP UNCOMPLAINING
EYES WIDE OPEN
ASKING WHY

VIII

IT WAS BLIND SLAUGHTER SLAUGHTER
BLOWS SHOUTS
SCREAMS HELP SAN NICOLA
SUFFERINGS BROUGHT US
PEASANTS TO THIS
ONE GRABBED ME
HIS NAILS IN MY FACE
HIS TEETH IN MY HAND
WHEN HE WENT DOWN
LIKE AN EMPTY SACK
ROSA HE CALLED OUT
ROSA

IX

WITH MY NEW SICKLE
STILL SPARKLING
ONE BLOW WAS SUFFICIENT
ON THE FEATHER-SOFT NECK OF PASQUALINO
SON OF THE RENT-GATHERER
FAT BLOOD-SUCKER AND SWAMP-SNAKE
I USED
SICKLES SCYTHES AND KNIVES
TO REAP WHEAT CORN HAY
FOR THOSE DAMNABLE DOGS
LANDLORDS

X

I SOUGHT OUT THE BARON
LORD OF SOLLAZZO
BUT HE BOLTED INTO SOME HOLE
SON OF A WHORE
VENGEANCE AT ALL COSTS
VIVA LA LIBERTA
THOSE WHO DIE DIE
GENTRY LANDLORDS NEVER CHANGE
HIGHWAYMEN
HEARTLESS AND GODLESS BEASTS
ALL THAT GRIEVES ME IS LEAVING SERAFINA
I HAVE NO FEAR
OF DEATH OR PRISON

XI

FUCK ITALY
BUGGER THE KING
AND DAMN GARIBALDI
JUDAS THE COLONEL
WHO DISARMED US
VIVA LO POPOLO
VENGEANCE UPON VENGEANCE
A BITTER FATE AWAITS ANY MAN
WHOM ILL LUCK BRINGS BEFORE ME
SAYING ONE KING ONE MOTHERLAND
I WILL DO TO HIM WHAT I DID
TO THE NOTARY BARTOLO
HEAD OF THE ROBBER GANG
WITH MY BARE HANDS I TORE HIM APART
AND CHOPPED IN TWO
THE STONE OF HIS
HEA   RT

XII

THIS IS THE TRUE STORY
OF WHAT OCCURRED IN ALCARA
IN MAY AND JUNE
OF THE YEAR SIXTY
TOLD BY THE PEOPLE
WHO MADE IT
WRITTEN WITH CHARCOAL
ON STONE
BY MICHELE FANU OF SAN FRATELLO
WHO FROM BEING MONK BECAME FARM-HAND
    IF YOU ENTER INTO
    THIS TWISTING DUNGEON
    KNOW WHAT HAPPENED IN THIS PLACE
    AND HOLD YOUR PEACE
    BEAR WORD WHEN YOU LEAVE
    THAT THE DAY WILL COME
    WHEN THE RAGE OF THE PEOPLE OF ALCARA
    OF BRONTE TUSA AND CARUNIA
    WILL NOT LEAVE ON THE FACE OF THIS EARTH
    SO MUCH AS THE SEED OF
    SERVANTS AND MASTERS
        THE OWL THE FALCON AND THE CROW
        ALL THREE WILL ONE DAY CROAK THEIR MOURNFUL
                          SONG

        TO CURSE SAINT BLAISE
        MUSKET AND DAGGER
        DEATH TO ALL RICH MEN
        THE POOR FOLK CRY
        FROM THE DEPTH OF THEIR ABYSS
        BREAD LAND
        THE ORIGIN OF ALL IS THERE
        THE UNENDING HUNGER
                FOR
                LIBERTY

APPENDIX ONE

A celebrated deliberation, at least as paradox

or

Murder triumphant

(Palermo, Carini Printers, trade mark Guttemberg – Entrance to the National Theatre, San Ferdinando – ground floor, right – 1860)

Volume 54 of the *Giornale d'Italia per gl'Italiani*, volume 187 of the *Diario d'Arlecchino* and volume 9 of the *Cittadino* have reported a decision reached by the High Court of Messina (by a majority of three to one) on the case led by the State Prosecutor Interdonato. With this verdict, in violation of the law of the land and in flagrant disregard for the rights of the individual and of society, the sentences previously handed down on the rebel band convicted of crimes against the gentry of Alcara Li Fusi, and of depredations against public charities, were annulled, and those found guilty of massacre, pillage and robbery in the town set at liberty.

These announcements have, however, passed unobserved, the Government has stood idly by and the public has waited in vain for some measure to reassert the claims of justice.

To prevent the Government from pleading ignorance of the facts, to furnish the public with a full account of the case and to make the King himself aware of what manner of man has been entrusted with the life and liberty of the citizenry and of public tranquillity in this part of Italy, we propose, without further expenditure of words, to publish in full the documents which demonstrate the extent of the injustice, indeed violence, which has been perpetrated.

On the 17 May in Alcara Li Fusi, a horde of scoundrels, motivated by the venom of private enmities and by the temptation of easy gain, murdered those of the gentry who fell into their hands, ransacking their possessions and thieving from the public coffers.

The Special Commission at Patti, informed of these events by the Dictatorial Decree of 9 June 1860, acting under emergency procedures but observing the normal facilities of pleading and legal debate, issued the following verdict:

IN THE NAME OF HIS MAJESTY VICTOR EMMANUEL
KING OF ITALY

In the year eighteen hundred and sixty, on this day 18 August, in the town of Patti.

The Special Commission of Patti composed of His Excellency

Crisostamo Gatto, President of the Court, Dr Enrico Lo Re, Dr Gaetano Bua, Judges, Dr Lodovico Fulci, Judge Rapporteur, and Dr Basilio Milio, Judge appearing as Advocate Fiscal,

Was convoked to pass judgment on:

Salvatore Oriti Gianni – Antonino Di Nardo Carcagnintra – Giuseppe Sirna Papa – Salvatore Artino Martinello Guzzone – Vincenzo Mileti Carcavecchia – Salvatore Fragapane Malandro – Nicolo, Giuseppe and Gaetano Vinci – Nicolo Santoro Quagliata – Michele Patroniti – Rosario Parrino Gruppo – Nicolo Romano Mita – Salvatore Cogita Calabrese – Gaetano Casta Caco – Giuseppe Sguro Mantellina – Nicolo Zaiti Scippatesti – Antonino Artino Inferno – Nicolo and Serafino Di Naso Milinciana – Carmelo Serio – Giuseppe Tramontana – Nicolo Tomasello Formica – Nicolo Calderone Sammarcoto – Don Ignazio Cozzo – Don Nicolo Vincenzo Lanza – Carmelo Cottone – Giuseppe Palazzolo Capizzoto – Nicolo and Salvatore Mellino Cucchiara – Santi Oriti Misterio – Pietro Ridolfo – Gaetano Catullo – Giuseppe Imbriciotta Zisi – Basilio Restivo Attinelli – Antonino Di Nardo son of Saverio.

CHARGED

With riot, murder and pillage in the township of Alcara and against the class of the gentry of that town; of conspiracy to assault, injure and murder the persons of Vincenzo Artino, Giuseppe Bartolo, Ignazio Bartolo, Salvatore Bartolo, Giuseppe Lanza, Luigi Lanza, Salvatore Lanza, Francesco Lanza, Gaetano Gentile, and Francesco Papa; of theft and damage to their possessions, of theft and damage to the archives of the aforesaid Notary Bartolo and to those of the Local Council, of theft and damage to the secular charities, to those of the convent of nuns and of the priest, Don Giuseppe Franchina [. . .].

All in terms of articles 130 and 131 of the Criminal Code, and in accordance with the citation of Judge Milio acting in his capacity as Advocate Fiscal.

Having heard the report prepared by the Judge Rapporteur, Signor Fulci,

Having read the proceedings of the case,

Having listened to all witnesses according to due process of law,

Having considered the address to the Court by the Advocate Fiscal,

Having listened to the pleas made by the accused through their respective Defence Counsels,

The Commission, at the termination of the public hearing, holds the following facts established:

The anarchy which occurred in Alcara on the 17 May and on approximately forty days subsequent thereto was not the consequence of random circumstances arising fortuitously in the course of the general uprising by all Sicily in pursuit of her rights, but the product of a preconceived, malevolent conspiracy by certain parties (for the most part artisans and peasants), whose purpose was the murder of a number of leading figures in Alcara. This number was increased in accordance with the private interests of individual conspirators, with the result that the aim came to be the slaughter (with few exceptions) of the entire upper class in that town.

The causes of this iniquitous conspiracy were, for certain parties, a virulent hatred and vindictiveness occasioned by previously endured vexations; the hope and wish for the annihilation of creditors so as to obtain release from the debts with which they were burdened; a wish which combined in many with the hope of reobtaining those goods which through the vicissitudes of fortune, the terms of a contract or the judgement of a magistrate they had previously lost or been compelled to cede; and finally, the hope of enriching themselves by theft in the course of the general, premeditated plunder.

The outcome of this abominable plot was the murder of ten gentlemen and one bailiff, including in that number various individuals respected for their civic and literary merits and certain young people whose tender years should have guaranteed their innocence. They were slaughtered by gunfire or axe blows, were beaten to death or butchered like sheep, and each one while dying or when already dead, whipped with various weapons, mutilated, trampled on, stripped of every item of clothing, appallingly disfigured by the holding of burning papers in the face, and finally, by a barbaric injunction, denied Christian burial. Other consequences were the destruction by arson of legal archives, of every charter and document in the Council Chancellery belonging to the Council or to Charitable Bodies; theft of substantial sums, part in specie part in credit notes, from Council coffers; forced entry into various gentlemen's houses with the theft of sums of money, credit pledges, jewellery, gold and silver objects, as well as the incineration of registers of credit, and of every document pertaining to private possessions; the devastation, made widespread and systematic following the intervention of anarchists, of fruit crops in the fields; the appropriation of houses and farms previously subject to court order; the taking, through voluntary disposition, established procedure or private act, of sums of money for use in bribery, the whole combined with menaces to life and property, arbitrary arrest and every other form of unlawful outrage; all these actions executed to the cry – *Viva Vittorio Emmanuele, Viva Garibaldi* – and in the shadow of the banner of regeneration, which had previously served to disarm opponents and claim credit for victories. These acts were planned as the first in a campaign, had not fortuitous circumstances intervened, and were intended as forerunners of a series of inhuman crimes, some of which later were carried out, and others, by the mercy of God, not committed.

The now accused having been apprehended, and being in the hands of Justice.

The facts in general being ascertained in said fashion.
The President of the Court formulated the following

QUESTION

Is it established that the accused, viz.: Don Ignazio Cozzo, Salvatore Oriti Gianni, Antonino Di Nardo Mileti Carcagnintra, Giuseppe Sirna Papa, Salvatore Artino, Vincenzo Mileti Carcavecchia Spinnato, Salvatore Parrino Tanticchia, Salvatore Fragapane Malandro, Nicolo Vinci son of the late Vincenzo, Nicolo Santoro Quagliata, Michele Patroniti [...] having been duly notified in accordance with law, are guilty of riot, murder and pillage in Alcara against the class of the gentry, as outlined in the aforementioned citation of the Advocate Fiscal?

THE COMMISSION

Considering [...].
On the basis of the considerations outlined above, as regards the question thus formulated, declares unanimously that

IT IS ESTABLISHED

[...]
Having thus resolved the questions of fact, the Commission proceeded to the passing of sentence. They condemned some of the accused to the supreme penalty, others to prison sentences, but, tempering the severity of the law, they commended some of those sentenced to death to the clemency of the Dictator.

Some of the accused were still in hiding, but this notwithstanding, they made every effort to obtain liberation; the Commission was deaf to their appeal, but not so the State Prosecutor (Signor Interdonato), who at the close of the sitting of the Special Commission, betook himself to a session of the High Court in Messina.

A petition had been delivered to him in which the fugitives requested inclusion in the act of amnesty signed in Naples on the 19 October. They themselves were fully aware that no other amnesty could be relevant to their condition. It should have been simple enough to establish that an amnesty covered crimes of blood committed in the course of the insurrection and occasioned by the insurrection could scarcely be applied to robbery and property crimes motivated by greed and the desire for revenge. Nevertheless, the State Prosecutor was unable to see this point with any clarity and felt it appropriate to place his doubts before the Government, thus: 'Do the terms of the amnesty apply only when the two conditions are met simultaneously, i.e. if the crimes were committed during the insurrection and occasioned by the insurrection?'

The Government did indeed condescend to reply to that doubt, even though it might well have chosen not to do so. However the terms of its reply, published in the *Giornale Officiale*, nos 161-5, could be reduced to this statement – Where the words are clear, no interpretation is required.

Having failed at the first attempt, Interdonato did not lack the effrontery to try another tack. Since the Government would have no truck with trade in disreputable favours, he applied instead to the courts. A fresh appeal was launched in which the request was made that the prisons be opened and the chains be removed from those convicted of the murders, assaults, robberies in the civil war in Alcara, all on the basis of the Decree of 17 October 1860, in which Garibaldi, with great political wisdom, declared null and void all accusations or convictions handed down by the Bourbon courts against those who had striven to overthrow the discredited despotism.

Well! Who would credit it? The State Prosecutor surrendered to this notion, and lodged an appeal which had the effect of confusing generous sentiment with vile passion, noble-mindedness with infamy, the liberal with the assassin.

[...]

A Procurator General was thus asserting that when Depretis, the representative of Garibaldi, Dictator of Southern Italy, stated that those actions categorised as political offences during the Bourbon occupation should not be subject to criminal action, but should render the individual in question meritorious in the eyes of our common mother Italy, he was turning a friendly smile in the direction of the thief, he was shaking the hand of the murderer, he was sanctifying robbery, murder, massacre, plunder, civil war . . . God in Heaven! Was this Garibaldi's intention? Are these (thieves, murderers, arsonists) the beloved sons of our common mother Italy? How can anyone so revile this sacred land as to make it the loving mother of the dregs of humanity?

A Procurator General avers that massacre, devastation, plunder in Alcara helped overthrow the Bourbon regime . . . a disturbing revelation. Does he believe that, in order to overthrow a detested government, theft and plunder are required? Does he believe such acts necessary? Does he imagine them in the least permissible? Let us, if he knows no liberals of any other stamp, grant him this last point. But when exactly did the Decree of 21 August legitimise ferocious acts committed in the name of overthrowing the Bourbon regime? The Decree talks exclusively of sentences handed down by tribunals for acts 'which during the Bourbon occupation were considered political crimes.'

No Bourbon court sat in judgement of the events of Alcara. The case was presided over by tribunals set up by the Dictator – revolutionary tribunals. The Public Prosecutor is guilty of appalling confusion, terrifying confusion [. . .].

It is the Procurator General, and only the Procurator General, who has confused thieves, a plague in society, with martyrs for liberty, a worthy object of veneration and respect [. . .].

Society has been mortally wounded by this decision. Are there legal remedies to hand? I do not know.

The Government plans to afford judges freedom of action, and in this it does well, but this faculty must be accorded to good, balanced, judicious magistrates. When, however, liberty becomes licence, when the magistrate betrays his mission, and when, instead of protecting society, he injures it; when the guardian of the law openly and brazenly violates it, there is only one remedy open to the Government – it must recall the judge, examine him, and if what has been advanced here is the truth, it must judge the judge, punish him, since by correcting a fault in one, it will offer an example to the others!

Palermo, 18 December 1860.

Luigi Scandurra

APPENDIX TWO

The township Patti, Province of Messina, town register, year 1860. Death certificate of Giuseppe Sirna Papa.

Order number 171 (one hundred and seventy one)

The year eighteen hundred and sixty, the twenty-first day of August, fourteen hundred hours.

There appeared before us, Giuseppe Natoli Calcagno, President and Chief Officer of the Council of Patti, District of Patti, Province of Messina:

Giovanni Campione, aged forty-two, profession grave digger, citizen of the Kingdom, domicile Strada San Michele, and Francesco Fallo, profession as above, citizen of the Kingdom, domicile as above.

Both declared that on the twentieth day of this month, year 1860, at eleven hundred hours, Giuseppe Sirna, aged twenty-six, profession farm labourer, domicile Alcara, son of Giuseppe, profession farm labourer, domicile as above, whereabouts of mother unknown, being under sentence of death by firing squad, was executed in the square of San Antonio Abate.

In fulfilment of the requirements of law, we betook ourselves with the aforesaid witnesses to the place where the now deceased was lying, and certified his physical death. We have therefore caused the present act to be drawn up and duly inscribed in the two relevant registers, having had the day, month, year read out to the witnesses in the prescribed form.

The witnesses declared themselves unable to write.

Giuseppe Natoli Calcagno

APPENDIX THREE

Proclamation of the Pro-dictator Morlini

ITALIANS OF SICILY

On acceding to power, I told you – your history obliges you to be great!

The time has come when it behoves you to prove yourselves such!

To hasten the accomplishement of your destinies, I have within the last few days chosen for you a path already trodden, to the applause of all Europe, by other peoples of Italy. And I chose it because it had the approval of the Dictator, because it led to a solemn pact of conciliation and peace, because it did not exclude the successive application of another principle of which I have always been a fervent supporter.

Today new events have altered the conditions of days past.

Away with hesitation!

Our task is to create Italy with concord.

ITALIANS OF SICILY

From the ballot boxes where on the 21st your future will be decided, ensure that this heart-felt message goes out to the peoples of the Peninsula: in Sicily there is no more division.

This will be for Garibaldi the strongest proof of your affection: it will be my greatest comfort as I take my leave of you.

Palermo, 15 October 1860.

Morlini
Pro-dictator

Translator's Afterword

THE AUTHOR

Vincenzo Consolo was born in 1933 in the village of Sant'Agata di Militello, on the north coast of Sicily, near the Madonie Mountains and the town of Cefalu where the action of this novel occurs. He spent his formative years in Sicily, but left in 1952 to attend university in Milan. Thereafter, as has been the case with such other Sicilian writers as Giovanni Verga, Vitaliano Brancati and Elio Vittorini, his life has been divided between the mainland and Sicily. It was during his days at university that the intention to become a writer took root. Although in those days of post-war neo-realism it was virtually an article of faith that the task of the writer was to reflect urban or industrial life, Consolo's ambition was to reflect 'Sicilian peasant experience', but not in creative fiction so much as 'in a sociological genre of writing, which could be easily communicated'.

After graduating, he returned to Sicily and took up a post as a teacher. His first novel, *La ferita di aprile* (The Wound of April), was published in 1963. 'When I began writing my first book, my intentions and convictions went one way but my passions and instincts carried me another. The story was not of the realistic-observation type, but metaphorical and autobiographical; the writing was not logical and referential but strongly transgressive and expressive.' The novel featured a group of boys attending a college run by a religious order, but in retrospect it became clear that the book was in many ways Consolo's 'Portrait of the Artist as a Young Man'. The book was respectfully but not enthusiastically received. It brought Consolo into contact with Leonardo Sciascia, and the two remained close friends until the latter's death.

He returned to Milan in 1968 to work with RAI, the Italian broadcasting authority, and still lives there. He seems to have undergone some kind of block after the publication of his first novel, and although the first chapter of *The Smile of the Unknown Mariner* was published in a magazine in 1969, the completed novel was published only in 1976. It was an immediate success, and established Consolo as one of Italy's leading writers. Subsequently, he has written several other works, winning the Strega Prize in 1992 with *Nottetempo* (Night-time), a novel dealing with the residence of Aleister Crowley in Cefalu. The author regards this book as forming a diptych with the present novel. Consolo has also written for the stage and is a frequent contributor to newspapers on both cultural and political subjects. He has been active in anti-Mafia campaigns, and has been outspoken in his attacks on Umberto Bossi and the Northern League. His work has now been translated into most European languages, but this is the first translation to appear in English.

THE NOVEL

'Sicilian literature,' as Vincenzo Consolo told one of his interviewers, 'is a literature of the margins, with precise lineaments of its own. Its themes are social and historical, scarcely ever personal. Even Verga and Pirandello paid their dues to history. This historical aspect has always been more marked in the west of the island. I was born in an anodyne zone, half way between the Province of Messina and the Province of Palermo. I chose the second. I chose history.'

As he observed, it was a choice made by many Sicilian writers, whose motivation was to find in the past an explanation of the present. The history of Sicily with its lengthy catalogue of invaders, from the ancient Greeks to the Allies in 1943, is not short of dramatic or tragic episodes which could transfer easily to the page or stage, and there are popular novelists – and Hollywood scriptwriters – who have fully exploited this wealth of material. However, for the major writers in the Sicilian literary tradition the historical novel was never merely the costume-drama or the exotic tale set in colourful surroundings, but an attempt to answer the question most cogently and plaintively formulated by Leonardo Sciascia – Why is Sicily as it is? Why, in other words, has Sicily become identified everywhere as the land of the most brutal form of gangsterism known to Europe? Why has Sicily suffered down the centuries from oppression, injustice, poverty and exploitation? Why has Sicily known only the dark side of every European experience? Why has Sicily been, as Lampedusa put it, the home of civilisations which, however splendid, were always imposed by outsiders, and not created by Sicilians themselves?

Sicilian literature has always been extremely, almost neurotically, self-obsessed. It may be that such a self-obsession is a mark of the small, 'marginal' nations like the Irish, the Catalans, the Czechs, the Scots, who have been the object of history and never its subject. In their quest for self-understanding, Sicilian novelists have focused on a limited number of key moments when choices were made, options were open and courses were set. Among such moments, none was of greater significance than the landing of Garibaldi and his Red Shirts in Marsala in 1860. In the old history books, this event is recounted in stirring, glorious terms as representing the unification of Sicily with mainland Italy and the opening of modern Sicilian history. Sterner historians debate the extent to which it also marked the fall of the aristocracy and absolutism, the advent of liberalism, the coming of the bourgeois revolution – and the emergence of the mafia. From the most divergent angles, 1860 has provided the theme for much of the most significant Sicilian historical writing – for Verga's short-story *Liberty*, for De Roberto's novel *The Viceroys*, for Pirandello's single historical novel, *The Old and the Young*, for Tomasi di Lampedusa's *The Leopard*, for Sciascia's novella *The Forty-eight* and his play *The Mafiosi*, as well as for the present book by Vincenzo Consolo.

Consolo creates his own style of historical novel but, in the best traditions of the genre, he mingles people and events from history with characters and incidents of his own creation. Mandralisca was a nobleman from Cefalu, whose grand marble tomb still stands in the church of San Francesco in the main street of the town. Near by is the museum which bears his name, and which houses his collection of coins, shells and paintings. Its principal exhibit is the portrait by Antonello which provides the title and leitmotiv to this novel. Mandralisca's principal passion was the study of the 'terrestrial and fluvial malacology' of Sicily, and his work on this subject is, apparently, still of value today. He was a deputy in the 1848 Sicilian House of Commons and later in the first Parliament of the Kingdom of Italy. He must have known Giovanni Interdonato, who was also a member of these two assemblies, as well as holding office during Garibaldi's Dictatorship in Sicily. There are records and archives which mention by name several of the peasants active in the uprising in Alcara, some of whom were later executed.

Consolo is meticulous in his researches, and his novel conforms to the test of the historical novel laid down by Lukács – whether the characters are so imbued with a sense of their own time as to appear inseparable from it. However, the accurate reconstruction of the past is not the only, or even the central, point of his style of historical novel. The essential differentiation between the costume drama and the genuine historical novel is, in the terminology Consolo employs himself, the presence of 'metaphor' or, more precisely, the construction of the entire novel as one overall metaphor. His supreme model remains the nineteenth-century writer, Alessandro Manzoni, author of *I promessi sposi*, the greatest historical novel in Italian.

> The lesson of Manzoni lay in the metaphor. We always asked ourselves why Manzoni set his novel in the seventeenth rather than in the nineteenth century; not merely from his passion for justice, but to provide the distance needed for his overarching metaphor. Manzoni's Italy seems indeed eternal, inextinguishable.

Consolo's ambition is not so much to create an eternal Italy but to provide images projected towards the present. The past requires to be read, but can be read only in the light of the present, and indeed the ultimate value of the historical novel lies in the greater clarity with which, through its medium, problems of the present can be considered. In Consolo's words:

It goes without saying that it was neither Garibaldi nor Bixio that interested me, but something else; it was the topics debated then, in the Seventies, which did interest me – the intellectual face-to-face with history, history and literature, the value of writing, the fate of those who have neither the capacity nor the possibility of expressing themselves and who have always carried the burden of history, the move beyond reason and irony by means of creative imagination... these were the themes of the novel, which aimed to be new and original from the structural and linguistic point of view.

Consolo is not the first to overturn the grand myths of the Risorgimento, but he is the first to focus on the marginal figures who were casually crushed in the making of history. His assessment of 1860 reopens a deep ambiguity implicit in the Risorgimento process. The English historian Denis Mack Smith, in his biography of Cavour, wrote that Cavour's aim in the Risorgimento was to achieve a 'conservative revolution', a revolution, that is, which would alter the political complexion of Italy without affecting the social and economic relations between the classes. In *The Leopard*, the young nobleman, Tancredi, has some comparable objective in mind when he justifies his decision to side with the Risorgimento forces with the much quoted words 'If we wish everything to remain the same, everything must change.' However, not all those who supported the Risorgimento were inspired by those limited, and cynical, aims. For some the social revolution which the potentates wished to check was the most cherished objective. The invasion by Garibaldi offered the peasantry of Sicily the prospect of the realisation of ancient dreams – the reform of the system which kept them landless, the division of the grand aristocratic estates, the redistribution of wealth, the prospect of an end to the poverty which had been their only experience of life. Unification of Sicily with Italy was an abstract goal, and over a century later the anti-Mafia crusader Danilo Dolci found many Sicilian shepherds and peasants who had still never heard of Italy.

Sicily had been in a state of unrest since the ending of the Napoleonic wars, and the arrival of Garibaldi triggered revolts in many Sicilian towns, as is recorded by Mack Smith in his magisterial *History of Sicily*. Of these, the best-known was the uprising in the town of Bronte, the subject of Verga's story. The revolt in that town was given a special virulence by the bitterness felt by local people over the gift by the Bourbon King of the best land in the locality to Lord Nelson, in gratitude for his contribution in safeguarding the Bourbon dynasty during the Napoleonic wars. (It is a curio of literary history that the snobbish desire of the Yorkshire clergyman, the Revd Patrick Brunty, to associate his family with Nelson led him to change his name, and give the name of the Sicilian town to the women who became known as the Brontë sisters.)

The rebels believed they were interpreting Garibaldi's words and implementing his programme, but the risings in both Bronte and Alcara Li Fusi – the subject of this novel – were put down with savagery. In focusing on the peasantry and on their social and political aspirations, Consolo takes his distance from *The Leopard*, published in 1958, a little more than a decade before Consolo began writing his book. Lampedusa's novel enjoyed a success at home and abroad which had no parallel until Umberto Eco's *The Name of the Rose*, but did not meet with total enthusiasm in some circles. There was a refined sneer – 'It's not a Leopard – it's a dinosaur!' – which made the rounds of exponents of the 'nouveau roman' in those years, while various left-wing critics jibbed at the conservative politics of the patrician author. Sciascia's historical novel, *The Council of Egypt* (1963), was hailed as the Anti-Leopard, although Sciascia himself always denied any such polemical intention.

Consolo too denied that he had ever entertained any intention of entering into debate with Lampedusa, but there is a greater logic in regarding his novel as the Anti-Leopard. Even the points of contact are significant. The protagonists of the two novels are aristocrats and men of science. Prince Fabrizio Salina is an astronomer, who finds refuge from everyday concerns in his observatory, while Enrico Pirajno, Baron of Mandralisca, is dedicated to malacology, the study of molluscs. The Baron has none of the Prince's attitude of studied disenchantment with affairs of state. His neglect of matters political is a source of concern, to himself as much as to Giovanni Interdonato. His questioning, in the aftermath of the popular rising, of his motives reflects the Sartrean debates of the 1960s on 'commitment' and the duties of the intellectual, neither of which were of any concern to the prince–protagonist or the prince–author of *The Leopard*. The relationship between Mandralisca and Interdonato has some resemblance to the relationship between Fabrizio and Tancredi, while the scene of the dinner in Mandralisca's palace in the second chapter recalls the dinner in the Prince's summer palace in Donnafugata when Tancredi and Angelica meet for the first time.

However, the complex of political beliefs behind the two novels, and the view of history mediated by the two writers, are incompatibly opposed. Lampedusa was no admirer of the myths of the 'glorious Risorgimento', and indeed in his debunking of those legends stood close to the left-wing historians with whom he had otherwise little in common; but he saw history as a chronical of the doings of the captains and the kings. He loathed the new democratic liberalism which the Risorgimento embodied, seeing in it the death-knell not merely for the Bourbon dynasty in Naples, for which Prince Fabrizio had little love, but for the patrician *ancien régime* which the Bourbons represented. His novel unravels in the salons and ballrooms of the most self-consciously blue-blooded upper class of all Europe. The peasantry have no role in his scheme, and no presence in his novel except as valets and gamekeepers.

It is the refusal of the underclass to continue to occupy subaltern positions and the plight of the landless, dispossessed peasantry which lie at the very heart of Consolo's civic and political vision. While the army of Liberation is sweeping across Sicily, the people of Alcara pre-empt matters by rising to liberate themselves, not from a Neapolitan royal tyrant, but from the local landlords and from injustices experienced in their own life. Their belief is that their cause and that of Garibaldi's army were one and the same. Two conflicting visions of the scope and purpose of the Risorgimento in Sicily lie behind the seemingly trivial dispute between Turi Malandro, the farmworkers' leader, and Don Ignazio Cozzo over the appropriate code-word to bring the rebels onto the streets. 'Viva l'Italia!' is the suggestion of the well-heeled

Cozzo, while the radical representative of the dispossessed stands out for 'Justice!', a word whose implications are devastating for the life-style of Cozzo – and Prince Fabrizio.

Consolo's radicalism is comprehensive, dictating his narrative and linguistic choices as well as his political inquiries. He freely employs Sicilian dialect terms in conjunction with standard Italian words, making the language of all his novels unfamiliar to many mainland Italians. His aesthetics and linguistics move in tandem with his politics, in the sense that as writer he reasserts the dignity of peasant speech, while his peasant characters assert their claim for land and hence for dignity as human beings. There are no literal or metaphorical inverted commas around dialect words, nor are they restricted to direct speech. In this way, the language of the disempowered periphery is given the same value and prestige as the language of the centre, and a further basis of power is deconstructed. Consolo's language has been called 'Joycean', but the comparison is misleading, for while Joyce happily coined and constructed a lexicon of his own making, Consolo employs only words which have some basis in historical usage. Of itself, this gives him considerable scope, and he revels in the linguistic diversity of Sicily. The passage of the Arabs, the Normans, the Spaniards, as well as – in more remote times – of the Greeks and Romans, have left their mark on the dialects, as on the architecture, of the island. The language of the village of San Fratello, situated not far from Sant'Agate di Militello, held a special fascination for him. The population were descendants of the Lombards, who had invaded the island centuries before, but maintained an idiom of their own, spoken by the boy taken prisoner and tortured by Maniforti in his castle; it is also the language used in the last poem on the dungeon walls. Consolo's use of this language has no savour of antiquarian flavour, and its relationship with standard Italian is part of the way the people there regard themselves. Its imperilled status is a symbol of the uncertain survival of a distinctive way of life.

The sense of despair, both over injustice endured and over a way of life which is passing, permeates the novel. Consolo is a unique blend of traditional and modern – or even 'post-modern'. If the writer's inspiration is a blend of history, invention or

memory, as Nabokov maintains, it is the last which is predomin-
ant in his case. This deep need to remember and *conserve* lies
behind those lists, or litanies, of words interspersed throughout
the novel. They may all indicate the identical object, or at least
objects which are almost indistinguishable, but they are cata-
logued lest they be wholly lost to the historical memory. They
are also honed, arranged, ordered; so as to heighten their poetic
impact. Dialect vocabulary offers considerable advantages here;
a little knowledge is a liberating thing. As Hugh MacDiarmid
found, the writer who employs a lexis which has never had the
dignity of fixed, written form can wrench his vocabulary out of
context, give it a metaphorical import and even a sense it never
quite had before.

Metre, rhythm and the poetry of sound are matters of considerable importance to Consolo. On several occasions, he has intoned
against the commercialised, debased, contaminated language in
use in fiction as much as in the media, and has wondered whether
it will be possible to preserve a space for the novel which is, he
believes, threatened by other forms of narration which do not
aspire to, or merit the designation of novel. These twin concerns
merge in his choice of highly poetic diction. He aspires in his own
fiction to a language which has the quality and purity of prose
poetry, so as to defend the claims of the novel as art. As he writes:

> I believe that the way to find a new literary space is to bring the
> prose of narration closer to the poetic form – I say form, not
> substance – to confer on it a certain poetic dignity and render
> it less consumable. While remaining within secular confines
> myself, I say that it is necessary to move prose towards a more
> sacred, less commercialised aura.

His novels eschew the colloquial, clichéd, pedestrian speech of
daily life or of the written and spoken mass media – an idiom
deliberately chosen by some of his contemporaries – in favour of
an elaborate, crafted, semi-poetic style.

It is not only the choice of style which makes Consolo a 'difficult' writer. His writing makes complex, intense emotional and
intellectual demands of his readers. The narrative is deliberately
fractured and disjointed, and the novel is imbued with a very

contemporary scepticism – philosophical, aesthetic, political and
epistemological in nature – over history, narrative, language and
the conventional ways of representing events and human beings
in writing. The doubts over history are part of the intellectual and
moral development of the protagonist, who comes to see all history as a chronicle written by the privileged classes. Like a good
liberal, he places his trust in education, which will confer on
people the power that is language. In the novel, the only statement of history is made in the form of the graffiti scrawled on the
prison walls by the semi-literate prisoners.

The scepticism over narrative determines the structure of the
novel. One criticism frequently made on the book's first appearance was that it was 'constructed', or put together as a series of ill-
connecting episodes. Sciascia rebutted this charge, on the grounds
that it was unthinkable that a great book could be any less 'constructed' than a house. 'The *habitability* of a book depends on this
simple and indispensable fact – that it be constructed in accordance with rules of *habitability*. *Uninhabitable* books, that is books
without readers, are those which are not constructed; and today
they are legion,' wrote Sciascia.

Consolo refuses to narrate, or to tell a story in which one
episode follows naturally from another. His narrative is deliberately piecemeal, so that every chapter seems a self-contained
short-story. The recounting of the central historical facts on the
invasion and the risings in Cefalu in 1856 and in Alcara in 1860 are
conveyed by excerpts from (totally authentic) historical sources,
which are interspersed with chapters of invention. The reader of
the traditional novel would have expected an account of the disorder on the streets of Alcara to have constituted the climax of the
novel, but Consolo skips past it. The preparations and the aftermath are detailed but not the event itself. Fresh characters, like
that of the deranged monk, Frate Nunzio, who represents the
forces of anti-reason, make their appearance only when the narrative is well underway. 'I had no wish to write a nineteenth-
century style self-contained, well-rounded, sage or didactic historical novel, whose aim was entertainment or consolation,'
wrote Consolo. 'If I had, I would have contradicted the presup-
positions with which I departed. I exposed the fabric which lies

under the literary invention; I set out the historical documents between one episode and the next. In other words, I removed the colour from the fresco.'

In the absence of narration, the novel is a highly literary 'construction' or pastiche of images, recollections and quotations as well as of invention. Like Borges, Consolo gives the impression of writing in a library or gallery. There are certain common images, notably the image of the Antonello portrait, which represents reason and measure throughout, and the image of the snail shell, which comes to represent their opposite. The image of the shell is more pervasive than will be apparent to an English-speaking reader, since the Italian word *chiocciola* means both shell and spiral staircase, and so represents the prison in which the prisoners are confined after the uprising. Goya, who wrote that 'the sleep of reason produces monsters', is a presence throughout, most especially in the structuring of Mandralisca's observations in his Petition (Chapter 7), where individual sections bear the titles of etchings from the *Disasters of War*. There are many other echoes. The description of the 'conversion' of Peppe Smirna in *The Vespers* is a pastiche of a passage in Manzoni recounting a religious conversion, while the subsequent description of the landscape carries references to Millet's painting, *The Angelus*.

The novel is, then, a richly textured, literary and cultural product, but also a work of intense political, social and historical passion. It is not a cold, mechanically constructed work, but a work of deep humanity, made visible in the smile of the Unknown Mariner, a smile as ironic, mocking, enigmatic and bewitching as that of the *Mona Lisa*.

I am grateful to the author for his assistance in clarifying troublesome points. I am, once again, grateful to Sharon Wood for her many helpful suggestions. I am more indebted than I can say to Antonio Restivo, himself a native of the Madonie region in Sicily. Without his patient and generous help, the work could not have been done.

Joseph Farrell
Glasgow